I0684521

It's Complicated

Book Two
Scorned

By

Erika Renee Land

Copyright © 2017 by Ezarie Publishing LLC.

All rights reserved. No part of this book may be reproduced in whole or in part in any form, except by newspaper or magazine reviewers, who wish to quote brief passages in connection with a review. It may not be transmitted in any form or by any means without written permission of the author.

Erika Renee Land
wwww.erikaRland.com

ISBN 978-0-9852836-6-7

This book is a work of fiction. Names and characters and incidences either are the product of the author's imagination or are fiction and any resemblance to actual persons, living or dead, is entirely coincidental.

"Don't get angry because you got caught."

"Holding on to anger is like grasping a hot coal with the intent of throwing it at someone else; you are the one who gets burned."

— _Gautama Buddha_

Dedicated to

Dedicated to the most forgiving person I know. You are a beautiful star that illuminates my life.

Love you, Mom

Acknowledgments

Writing this book has been a journey, and there have been many people who have helped me accomplish publishing this book. While extending an encompassing thank you does not justify the gratitude I have for each of you, to avoid leaving anyone out, I am compelled to write an all-inclusive 'Thank You.'

Family, friends, colleagues, associates, my publishing partners, and the list goes on, I want to thank you for your encouraging words, reads and re-reads, designs, edits, and so much more. Thank you for believing in me and my dreams. Thank you for providing direction for my ideas and spaces for them to flourish, as fly by and random as they were at times. You all know who you are, so please accept this gracious THANK YOU.

To my mother, Renee Rhodes, there are not enough words. Without your love and guidance, Scorned may not have happened. Thank you for letting me know that as long as my decisions have merit, there will be light at the end of the tunnel.

I have love for you all.

E.R.L

Scorned

Introduction

I couldn't have imagined my first lesbian experience being like this. Currently, I'm in an elevator with a woman that I thought loved me. She has deceived me gravely, but right now, while looking at her, I don't know what to do. A part of me wants to talk it out, find out what happened because she can't be this malicious, the other part wants to strangle a bitch.

The first woman I've loved is not only engaged to another woman but also is in love with someone else on top of that. She has three lovers that I know of, and I don't know where I fall on the pyramid.

I give it to her, though. Laila Morriston is a master of deception. I don't know what was and what wasn't true in our relationship. Laila made me feel amazing and seemed to be a truthful person. From the moment I met her, I took her to be extremely honest. I didn't think she was capable of being with multiple people at one time, but I guess that's where I went wrong. Too often, we tend to underestimate others.

What goes around comes back around, though, and that's probably why she had to deal with Tasha stalking her ass. And thank goodness for that, because it probably wouldn't have come out that she is a – a – lying son of a bitch, yeah that's what she is. She likes to tell half the story, making her a liar.

This is the second time someone has crushed my feelings. However, I won't be devastated like I was when my ex-husband Xavier didn't leave me a pot to piss in. Oh no, she will not get the best of me. I'm saying it now, Laila Morriston has scorned Nadia York, but she won't get away with it. She's not going to get off scot-free and go live happily ever after...especially since I have given myself to her sexually.

1

Camille

I'm sitting at my desk when Jeremy runs in from the living room and tells me that my friend Laila is on the TV.

"What are you talking about son?"

"I was flipping through the channels and saw her."

I slam my laptop closed and tell him to turn on the TV in my office. After watching two minutes of commercials, the woman I've been in love with for the past six months appears. As she is entering the SWAT truck she turns around to look behind her, and the media catches her face plain as day. A still shot of her anguished face is plastered on the screen. My heart rate picks up and my palms become sweaty. I need to help her.

"Jeremy, get your jacket. We have to go."

"I was about to watch Animal Planet."

"Jeremy, now!"

"Fine."

I drop Jeremy off at his father's house and make it to Chinatown in about twenty minutes. I illegally park the car on a side street and try to get as close as possible to the Verizon center, but I'm stopped in front of the Gallery Place/Chinatown metro entrance because the crowd is too thick. I start tapping people on the shoulder and saying excuse me repeatedly as I weave through the crowd. I finally reach the yellow caution tape and ask the man standing next to me if he knows anything. He shakes his head and shrugs his shoulders indecisively.

I look toward the row of swat cars and I see Laila standing there, bent slightly forward in the black armor they've instructed her to wear. My eyes are drawn to her feet. The rain the past couple of days has softened the ground, causing her high heels to sink into the grass. *I've always liked her ankles.* I imagine the weight of the SWAT gear is throwing her balance off.

Flashes above my head draw my eyes upward. Multiple colors are moving quickly across the Verizon center's LED projection screen advertising the newest cell phone. I look back to the SWAT truck; Laila's back is facing me now. I look up at the screen again.

When the commercial is over Laila's face graces the screen, she's crying now. Mascara is running down her cheeks, and she is crossing and uncrossing her arms; she always does that when she's nervous, so no one will notice her hands trembling. Someone points toward the top of the building. Laila's eyes follow their pointing. Shock overcomes her face. I guess she's noticed that her face is amplified on the screen. She tries to shield herself away from the scrutiny by covering her face with her forearm. She is vulnerable right now, and it's being broadcast to the world. My eyes abandon the screen and focus on her again.

I watch her rock back and forth like a pendulum. Aloud I murmur, "Laila, honey, what is all this about?"

She turns and looks in my direction as though she heard me whisper like she knows I'm here to rescue her, to protect her by any means necessary. She bends over and removes her four-inch heels. Remembering I have a pair of her running shoes in my trunk, I race to get them.

When I come back, I make it two feet past the yellow tape before an officer stops me. I convince him and two other blue bloods that I'm her assistant. Eventually, they let me through. As I'm walking toward her, there's a commotion. The police are roughly escorting Tasha from the edge of the building. When I look back down, it's hard to spot

Laila amongst the scrambling crowd. If it weren't for the woman now standing beside her, I may have missed Laila's five-foot-two frame. The woman, who is wearing University of Maryland yellow, is holding my lover's hand. Their fingers are intertwined in a way that lets me know they are more than familiar with each other.

I loudly call Laila's name, pulling her attention away from the woman. Instinctively, she turns her head in my direction and scans the crowd. I call her name again, and she lets go of the woman's hand. When our eyes lock, Laila says my name in the shocked way you do when you're caught off guard. I hold out her running shoes so she can see them. I try to move closer, but the officer continues to block my way. Laila hurriedly walks toward me. When she reaches me, I grab her hand, ask her if she is okay, hand her the shoes and tell her I love her. For a moment, she tries to pull her hand away, but I don't let go until she says I love you back. She whispers it, barely moving her mouth, but she says it nonetheless. I gather myself and walk away to the back of the crowd.

* * *

Victoria, a.k.a Tori

"Tori, Tori, listen. Someone is about to jump from the Verizon center with a sign that says only Laila Morriston can save her."

"Get off my phone, Chris."

"Tori, I'm dead serious. I'm watching the news. Oh my god. They just showed her picture. Yep, that's her—short wavy hair, oval face, almond-shaped eyes. That's Laila, all right."

"What channel?"

"Four."

I hang the phone up and try to call Laila. She answers on the second ring and immediately starts talking.

"Honey, I can't talk right now."

"I'm coming down there."

"No, no, no, no, no. You're in no condition. I'll be home soon."

"What's going on, Laila?"

"I'm fine."

"Are you sure?"

"Tori, please. I don't have time for questions right now. Don't come down here."

She hangs up on me. I immediately call Christina back.

"Chris, come get me?"

"I'm already on my way."

I turn on all the TVs in the house, each to a different news station, and get dressed while waiting for Christina.

On one of the networks, a man being interviewed says he saw a woman walking back and forth and she keep sitting on the edge of the arena's roof, and

16

then she pinned a sign to the side of the building that read *Only Laila Morriston can save me.*

The anchor finishes the segment. "Police authorities have blocked off the area surrounding Chinatown, and have also evacuated businesses in the vicinity. The assailant seems to be focused only on a person named Laila Morriston, who we've been told is on the scene. We encourage everyone to stay clear of the area. We will be back shortly with updates on this situation, which will hopefully come to a peaceful conclusion soon."

Twenty minutes later, Christina rushes into the house. "Girl, what happened?"

"They got Tasha down. The replay should be on soon, they keep replying it." I respond.

"What's wrong, Tori?"

I walk her into the living room and rewind the DVR to Laila holding hands with another woman.

Taken aback, Christina says, "Oh, well, that could be her co-worker whose hand she's holdin'. She is a femme, and Laila doesn't like feminine women, right?"

Tears begin to fall. I fast-forward a couple of seconds to a woman telling Laila she loves her, and Laila mouthing the words back.

"Who is that?"

"That woman is a stud, Chris. How do you explain that? I... I..." Before Chris can answer my rhetorical question, I start to hyperventilate. Chris scrambles around the kitchen, looking for a bag I can breathe into.

"Calm down, hun. Don't get too worked up. Breathe for me."

Through gasps I utter, "Take me to Trey's house."

* * *

Nadia

I smile every time I run past this trash can. My heart remembers how I got over being nervous and spoke to a woman I was attracted to for the first time.

Something I hadn't felt before engulfed me. It was like, I saw how beautiful she was, and all of my energy shifted toward her. I wanted to see behind her Gucci sunglasses, to hear the elegantly dressed woman's voice, to experience the fragrance she wore that day. I needed to be near her.

It was eight months ago that I saw Laila sitting on a bench that is no longer here. I ran by her three times before I convinced myself to say hello. On my fourth pass, my pace, which had increased out of anxiousness, was staggered. As I came out of the right turn into the straightaway, I saw that the bench was empty. Disappointment, a feeling I've felt too often in my life, overwhelmed me. I stopped midstride and kicked a small rock. She was gone—I'd waited too long.

I always seem to make a decision to do something too late. I'm the walking version of a day late and a dollar short.

I started cursing and throwing a small temper tantrum by kicking at the dirt and the pebbles because, once again, my lack of action, being stuck in my head, had cost me, but then I saw her walking toward this trash can.

My mind flustered, I had no idea of what to say or do, so in the most awkward way, I approached her and stuck my hand out, said my name rushed, like a teenager, and two sentences later invited her for coffee. I'd like to say it was a surge of assurance driving me, but it was the fear of losing the interaction I thought I'd already lost.

For two years, I'd been itching to date a woman. My boss, Mrs. Spady, tried to set me up numerous times, but it never worked out. I was still healing from my divorce and emotionally unready. But when I saw her, I put all my reservations away—she was the one.

In the distance, I hear a church bell ring. I look at my watch and take off running. It's almost lunchtime. I'm having a solo lunch in Dupont Circle at Alero my favorite Mexican restaurant. I love their chicken soup. I sprint my last lap then go to my condo to spruce up and feed Bruce.

Before I can reach my door, I hear Bruce getting excited on the other side. I open the door slowly so it doesn't hit his nose too hard. This happens at least once a day because he likes to rest his head against the cold metal at the base of the door. He jumps up and places his paws on my shoulders. I rub my hand against his fur and say repeatedly, "There's my big boy!" My phone vibrates in the middle of our love fest, and I accept the call.

"You've reached Nadia."

It's my ex-husband. "Your little girl misses you."

"Don't start with me today, Xavier."

"What? It's the truth."

"Is she there with you?"

"Not exactly."

"I know she's not. You just like fucking with me." He pisses me off with these calls every day about nothing.

"Now, why would I do that?"

"Well, what other reason do you have to call me every day?"

The messed up thing is I have to answer his calls because it could be about our daughter Olivia. As my luck would have it, the one time I don't answer, something serious would be going on.

"I was just calling to make sure you're okay."

"I'm fine. Anything else?"

"Why are you so rude when I call?"

"Because you always call with nonsense."

"I call to make sure you're okay."

"You can do that through a text."

"Well, I figure that you probably miss the sound of my voice and--"

"Here you go."

"Well, you've got to miss something about me."

I sigh and softly shut him down. "I don't like who you've become."

"Well, you made me this way."

I get mad and yell. "I didn't do shit. You're always trying to blame me for your insecurities." I hang up the phone before he can respond. I wait a few minutes for him to call back, but he doesn't, so I shower and head to D.C.

While driving through DuPont Circle, the radio DJ interrupts my song to make a special announcement.

"If your name is Laila Morriston, please get down to H and Seventh Street as soon as possible. Again, if your name is Laila Morriston, please get down to the Verizon center now."

Wait! Did they just say Laila Morriston?

"We have breaking news, listeners. There is a woman holed up on top of the Verizon center with a sign that reads: *Only Laila Morriston can save me.* Right now, the D.C. police department says they do not know the woman's intentions, but they are deploying their Jumper squad just in case. So again, if you are, or if you know Laila Morriston, get her to the Verizon center ASAP. You can't write true life, people. You can't write true life."

I park in the nearest garage and call Laila. After an eternity, she answers.

"Laila, where are you? Have you heard?"

"I can't talk right now. I have to go."

"Well, I'm on my way down there, okay?"

"Yeah."

I get out of my car, run to the main level of the garage, and then to the nearest Metro entrance. I catch the train to Metro Center station, and then run four blocks up F Street to Eighth. The media and spectators are congregating.

I cross under the police tape, and I'm immediately stopped. I'm trying to explain to the officers that I'm Laila's lover when I see them escorting her out of a SWAT truck. I call her name while jumping up and down; she reaches her hand toward me, and they finally let me pass.

When I reach her, I try to sound light-hearted. "I knew something was wrong with that woman when I met her," Laila smirks. I grab her hand and try to comfort her. We hear someone from the crowd yell Laila's name. She looks to the left and then abruptly releases my hand. She looks back at me with an overly sincere expression and mouths "sorry."

I watch her run over to someone and grab a pair of shoes. I look up at the LED screen. As Laila tries to walk away, the woman grabs her hand and says what looks like the words *I love you*. Well honestly, I can't tell from this distance, but that's sure what it looked like. After a few seconds, the woman lets go of Laila's hand. When Laila turns to walk away, the woman bends over, wipes her hands across her face, and then squats as if she's overcome with anguish.

When she returns to me, I ask, "Was that Camille?"

She responds in a whisper, "She brought my shoes."

"Did she—" I stop myself from asking a question I don't want the answer to, an answer that may hurt too much. We stare at each other blankly.

The police urge us back to the SWAT truck. Laila keeps a safe distance between us as we walk.

Once inside the tactical truck, I place my hand on top of Laila's. "It's over, honey. Everything is okay now."

She smiles and shakes her head no while trying to hold back tears. She pulls her hand away from me and starts grinding her right thumb into the palm of her left hand. The detective is trying to talk to Laila, but she has zoned out, probably talking things over with herself. She does that a lot.

She mumbles that she has to go while frantically stripping out of the protective gear. Detective Williams tries to calm her, but she interrupts him and insists she must leave. He says he doesn't have the authority to let her go. They go back and forth for a couple of minutes.

Laila's frustration hits its peak, she looks at me and the detective, wipes tears from her face, and then bolts to the door.

The detective calls her name and gives chase; I follow behind them. Laila runs straight into the media, and they swarm her like a pack of bees. We push through the cameras and microphones to rescue her from the madness.

A few officers also intervene and help us make our way through the crowd. Once we are clear, Detective Williams comes over and tries to get Laila back in the SWAT truck, but again she says she needs to leave. Laila and Detective Williams come to a compromise—he'll visit her at home later for a follow-up. He walks us over to two officers leaning against their cruisers. Laila looks at me with tearful eyes, and I say what she doesn't want to, "We need both of them, so we can go our separate ways."

As Laila is getting into the back of one of the police cars, I realize that her life is more drama-filled than I first thought. *God, I wish I knew the events that led up to today.* I start biting my nails. *I love that woman, but I think... I think she's cheating on me.* I try to shake the thought, telling myself repeatedly that she's not like that, but I can't ignore what my eyes saw. I feel a hand softly grip my shoulder.

"Miss... Miss, it's time to go now." I turn and look at the female officer.

I give her half a smile and say okay.

She opens the car door while asking for my destination. I tell her Dupont Circle. While sitting in the back of the cruiser, my mind is stuck on what transpired between Tasha and Laila that would make Tasha climb on top of a fucking building.

Ten minutes later, the officer opens the cruiser door and I disappear into the parking garage. Not able to find my car, I start pushing the alarm button on my keychain. When I don't hear anything, I look around and realize I'm in the wrong garage. I become extremely frustrated and yell *fuck you* at the top of my lungs. It echoes back at me. Flustered, I sit on the curb so I can pull my shit together. A woman speaking on her cell phone pulls my attention away from the pavement.

As the woman passes, I notice she has on a pantsuit similar in color to the one Laila wore the first time we had lunch.

Eight months ago, when Mrs. Spady and I walked into Expected Architecture and I saw Laila from behind, I knew she was the woman I'd met the week before. Not because I noticed her cropped hair; it was her ass that I remembered. I'd been replaying the sway of her hips in my head all week, so when I saw her squat with her knees together, making her ass look perfectly round in her skirt, I knew it was her.

I wanted to drop a pen in front of her so she would kneel down again to pick it up. I looked over and saw Mrs. Spady shaking her head at me. I quickly straightened my posture and clothing when I realized my head was tilted in admiration. Before I knew what was happening, Mrs. Spady invited Laila to lunch.

Mrs. Spady was laughing at my giddiness on the ride to McCormick & Schmick's. I was antsy because I was going to ask her on an official date. I kept going over what to say, but it never came to me. While we were eating, I continuously had to remind myself not to stare at her. I couldn't believe that I had run into her again so soon. It was fate.

When she went to the bathroom, Mrs. Spady told me I should go "check" on her to make sure she was okay. I tried to contest it, but Mrs. Spady insisted, so the only choice I had was to shake the nerves, follow her to the bathroom, and ask her to go on a date with me later that night.

When she agreed, I was ecstatic. We finished lunch and Laila opted to go shopping with us instead of back to work. We ended up spending the rest of the day together.

After that, we started kickin' it regularly, and then one day I got the nerve up to kiss her. It was the most beautiful feeling I've experienced. Her lips were soft like tiramisu, and I felt like I was floating in a sea of bubbles.

I stand up and head toward the correct parking garage, trying hard to shake thoughts of Laila from my head. As I walk past the Chinese restaurant, I see that they are closing for the day. I look at my watch and realize it's almost 7:30 p.m. A kid on a skateboard rushes by and yells, "Look up lady." I grunt and decide to go see Mrs. Spady.

* * *

Laila

After having to go to three stores to find Tori some strawberries, I'm sitting here at the end of my block with my forehead planted against the warm leather of the steering wheel. *Okay, Laila, you've been parked under this tree long enough. Make a move. Turn left, park in the driveway, open the door, and apologize. It's not gonna be easy, but you have to do it. You made this bed, now it's time to lie in it.*

I start the car and wait for my neighbor to turn off the street before I take off. I don't want to be stared at any more than I have to be; I can't take the judgment. I lift my head and open my eyes when I no longer hear the engine groaning.

I look to my left and Christina, my dentist's secretary, has stopped her car under a light post. She's looking in my direction. I look at the clock. It's 8 p.m. She's taking her seat belt off. God, give me the strength.

I roll my window down a quarter of the way. Christina sticks a card through the window. "I just wanted to give you this," she says. I smile in acceptance. She taps her hand against the top of the car the way a parent would while saying good luck to a child. Then Christina trots back to her Nissan.

A cool breeze creeps into the car, giving me chills. I flip the plastic wallet-sized card over, give it half a glance, then toss it to the passenger side of the car. It hits the door then falls into that empty space between the seat and the door. Thank you, God, for the strength you are about to bestow upon me.

I drive to the house and open the door. Tori is upstairs, sleeping in the middle of the bed. She has thrown my pillows onto the floor. I go into the bathroom to sulk. A few minutes later, I hear a commotion. I go into the bedroom, and Tori is missing. I hear scraping across the floor, and I run downstairs. Tori has moved one of the recliners into the hallway, blocking me from fully descending the stairs.

Tori sits in the chair. I immediately start groveling. "Tori, I'm sorry. I thought you were asleep... I fucked up. None of this should have happened. You told me not to get close to Tasha, but I didn't listen, and she's gone and done this, embarrassing me, and the company, and you..." I look up to see her giving me a death stare. I break into a sob.

"Oh stop it, Laila. You don't get to stand there and cry. You don't get to play the victim. You created this mess and don't even want to own it."

"But I do. I just said I didn't listen."

She waves her pointer finger back and forth and shakes her head at me. "You know damn well what I'm talking about."

I struggle to straighten my face. "Tori? I..."

"Before you say something fucked up, you better take a moment to get your story straight." She puts her left elbow on her knee and her fist under her chin. "How long have you been in love with someone else?"

My washcloth, which I've been using as a form of security, slips from my fingers.

"Don't stand there with that stupid look on your face, like you don't know what I'm talking about. I saw you on the TV."

"Baby, it's not what you think."

"Oh, so now you're trying to play me for a fool?"

"NO. Fuck."

"See, I knew you were going to be on some bullshit when you got here. I knew it from the moment you stepped through the door."

"Tori, let's just take a moment to —"

"We're not taking a moment for shit; you're getting my blood pressure up."

"Look, look, I don't know what to say. I don't want to own my shit."

"Well, at least you're honest about something."

"That was supposed to be in my head."

"Well, it fucking came out ya mouth."

"Shit, umm, Tori I know what you saw but —"

Tori starts breathing heavily and rubbing her hand across her belly. Not in the way a woman does when she is coddling her unborn child, but like she is trying to ease the pain away.

"Are you fucking kidding me right now? Like I didn't see you on TV with everyone else in Maryland, telling someone else that you love them... You know what? Don't worry about it; come to the fucking living room. I'm about to show you because I DVR'd it."

I rush down the stairs and drop to my knees. "Tori, I'm sorry."

"You know what, Laila, forget about that I'm not about to go through this with you anymore."

"Baby, no!"

"I'm done, Laila. You hear me? Done."

"So, you get to do all these things behind my back, but now you're trying to leave, just gonna walk away?"

"But you forgave me for that."

"Well, the scars are still there. Literally."

"Un-fucking-believable! I have done everything I can to atone for that, Laila."

"Even now, I don't know what's going on with you and Christina. Why was she leaving here?"

Tori throws her arms into the arm and walks over toward the TV. "Don't try to change the subject Laila; you're so good at that."

"I'm not. That's a legitimate question."

"She texted, asking If I saw what happened. I told her to come pick me up so she could take me to you, but you didn't need me after all did you."

"So what does she just come over when she feels like it?"

"I just told you I invited her and she is my friend, she can come over anytime just like Trey can."

I roll my eyes. Tori says, "Nothing is going on between us."

"I've heard that lie before."

"I'm not lying, and how did you turn this around on me? You always do that; make me feel like shit when you are in the wrong."

"Not my intention. It's just really strange that she popped up as your best friend out of the blue."

"Oh my god. You are a piece of work, Laila."

"You think I wanted all of this to happen? You think I wanted to cause all of this pain?"

"I don't know what to think."

I mumble, "You're the reason all of this happened, anyway."

"What'd you say?"

"Nothing!"

"No, say it. Say the reason, Laila."

"Victoria, let it go."

"No, tell me what the reason is. I need to know why you completely fucked up our relationship."

I whisper, "I thought you were cheating on me, again."

Tori's face drops, "Well, I hope you found some satisfaction."

I wipe my nose with my forearm. "I didn't, and I'm sorry. None of this should be happening."

She looks away from me. "You're damn right, it shouldn't."

I am full-blown crying. "Tori... do you think we can get past this?"

She rolls her eyes and ignores my question. "Sleep away from me tonight."

I don't fight her. I step past her and gather my things and turn to leave.

"Damn it, Laila, inside the house."

I stop gathering my things and realize the gravity of what my leaving would mean. I always take what she says at face value when I know she is not good at expressing herself. I turn around and look at her apologetically. She is silent. I follow her upstairs and turn toward the guest bedroom. When I look to my left just before entering the room, so that I can actually say the words 'I'm Sorry', I see her pony-tail disappearing. I stay quiet.

2

CAMILLE
April 7th, 2011

My call to Laila has failed twice already. Maybe that's a sign that I don't need to speak with her. Naw, fuck that. I'm calling again.

This time, she answers on the first ring. "Hey, Camille."

"You've gone and opened Pandora's Box, haven't you?"

"I'm sorry."

"Yeah, that's a lie. But whatever, no hard feelings. What are you doing?"

"Going to work. They sent a car this morning."

"Must be nice."

"I can't tell how you feel."

"Oh, I'm hurt like a motherfucker, but I can't make you a better person, so I'm gonna walk away before the hurt settles in too bad and I become angry."

"I'm sorry."

"No, you're not. If you had the slightest bit of conscience, you wouldn't have done this."

"Do you hate me?"

"No, but I feel sorry for you because the thing is—when people cheat, they feel double the pain because they lose both people, but you will have to deal with triple the hurt. We will move on, but guilt is gonna eat your ass up. And what have you accomplished? Other than a collection of orgasms? You're in more of a fucked-up place emotionally than before I met you. It does suck, though, because I fell for you. I wanted to experience the future with you. Now, I have to reflect back on all the things that could have been signs that I ignored. I have to figure out why I ignored the signs, why I was so blind to your antics, why I was so eager to give my love that I fell for all this fuckery."

"I'm sorry, Camille."

"I know, and you don't have to say it anymore. We're done."

I get frustrated and hang the phone up before she can respond. Eight months ago, Laila strolled into my life and set a piece of me on fire. Now it's over. I wipe the tears from my eyes.

* * *

Eight Months Earlier

Before taking the main stage, every dancer is required to take a shower in the waterfall behind the bar. It keeps everyone fresh and gives the illusion of a dancer in the tropics. The patrons love to gaze through the thick veil of water at the women seductively rubbing bubbles on themselves. It's like you know they are naked, but the water provides some mystery. That's also the only place you get to see the women fully naked.

I usually drift into my own world and ignore the customers while I'm in here, but when I turn my head toward the bar, a beautiful woman with a fade haircut to die for is standing there. I rise onto my tippy toes to get a better view through the strip of unfrosted glass. I can't take my eyes off her. She stretches her manicured hand out to grab the Razzle Dazzle Punch she ordered. I know it's a Razzle because I have memorized most of the drinks' colors. I have to keep an eye out for underage drinkers who try to swap drinks with those twenty-one and up. I don't want to lose my liquor license. Some of the liquid spills on the gorgeous woman's hand as she is taking the drink from the server. Jaycee put too much of the pre-made punch into the glass, but the woman okays it by mouthing "it's all right." After she takes a couple of napkins to clean her hands and the glass, she makes her way to one of the tables near the stage.

I rinse away the soap bubbles and exit the shower door that leads into the dressing room. I dry myself off as fast as I can, so I can make my way to the woman. Even though I'm a stripper, I'm also the owner of this establishment, so customer service is always at the forefront of my thoughts.

I walk up behind the woman and gently tap her shoulder. She jumps and pushes my hand away. She smells as beautiful as she looks, which makes me forget where I am for a moment. I usually refrain from becoming too familiar with the patrons, but I'm a little beside myself tonight so I ask for her name. She hesitates, eyeing me for second and then she says, "Robin."

The sound of her voice makes me wet. My impulse to get to know her intimately is steadily growing. I ask if I can give her a private lap dance, and she declines. I hope she'll change her mind once she sees Katana in action. I rarely meet people I'm attracted to in here, and I can't help wanting to know if she desires me, in more than that - I'm horny, as soon as I cum were done, kind of way.

I send my signal to the DJ, alerting him to call me to the stage when the current song ends. I need to show her my moves. Ten minutes later, her drink is still nearly full. She doesn't seem like the kind of woman accustomed to the after-hours lifestyle of partying until the sun comes up, so she could leave at any moment.

I don't know if being a stripper or business owner has led me to be as observant as I am, but she doesn't have that 'I need to floss' air about her, but I can tell she's well off, also, she's not a lingerer. The lingerers are always easy to spot. They try to hide in the darkest places of the club and move around often.

Inside the doors of this strip club, I am Katana, acrobatic stripper extraordinaire. In my daily life, I am Camille Jenkins-Borders, a single mother estranged from her family and trying to establish a legacy for myself. Hopefully, Katana will be able to entice this mystery woman into a lap dance, and Camille will keep her interested.

When I hit the stage, I do the most seductive dance I've ever performed. It's all for her, and she doesn't even know it. Usually, I entertain the mostly male crowd with flips, splits, and contortions to wow them with the many ways a woman can move her body. For Robin, though, I take my time feeling myself up, imagining her hands caressing every part of my body. I display the intensity of what I'm feeling through my movements. I stare at her seductively, waiting for our eyes to connect, and when they do, I feel like we get lost in each other. It's too overwhelming.

I throw my head back and let my body flow down to the floor. I lay on my back with my knees bent beneath me and slide my legs open and closed. I feel myself getting wet, which is something I thought I learned to control — it almost never happens when I dance. The DJ changes the song, and I let every acrobatic move I know rush from me furiously. I imagine an orgasm building between us. I can't take my eyes off her. She can't take her eyes off me. I think I can convince her to let me give her a private dance now.

Once the song ends, I cautiously make my way over to her by stopping and thanking the other tippers first. I don't want to seem too eager because she tipped me a couple hundred dollars. Well, I don't know exactly how much she left on the stage but it was a lot. My dancers don't pick up the money themselves; one of the security guards does. Once I'm close to her, I muster the courage to tell her to meet me for a dance. I whisper in her ear so I can smell her again.

Before she can tell me no, I do a move that drives men crazy. I bend over and put my ass on her crotch as I stand back up, and I clinch her shirt between my cheeks. It's hard to do this time because she's wearing a form-fitting shirt, but I manage to get it done. I think I got her with that. I go to the dressing room and try to wash away my wetness, then make my way to the private dance booth where she's waiting. As I walk into the room, I see her playing with herself.

When I designed this place, I made the private rooms so that you can see through the black glass doors when the interior light is turned on. This allows us to know that a room is empty, and it serves as a security measure for the dancers in case a customer gets out of hand. Robin is unaware of this and has her hands between her legs. I enter the room and turn the light off.

"Why did you do that?" She asks.

"Because you can see from the outside when the light is on."

"Shit, are you serious?"

"Yes, but relax. You can barely see in here. I don't think anyone saw you touching yourself," she chuckles.

Her head drops with embarrassment, and I cover my mouth with my hand.

I walk into the room and playfully alert her that I could see her touching herself. She becomes embarrassed. I turn the light off and ease her mind with my dance. As I slowly grind on her, something takes over inside me and I give into my own sexual pleasure, which seems to suddenly overpower me. I haven't had sex in years, and a long-buried desire rises out of me. I begin to ride her. She has me so aroused that I'm about to orgasm.

Suddenly, I'm cumming. Oh, shit. I can't stop. Fuck. "I want to fuck you until the sun comes up two days from now," I say. She grabs my ass and pulls me into her hard. I thrust my hips forward and throw my head back, almost making my wig come off, but I don't care. "Robin . . . I'm . . . going to . . . cum." I start shaking as I pull myself forward and collapse onto her shoulder. It feels like my pussy is pouring. *What the fuck is she doing to me?*

The after-effects of my orgasm are short lived as I realize how many rules I've broken. Panic sets in, and I need to think of something quick. I apologize about five times and ask her to meet me by the pool tables in five minutes. She agrees, but it takes me longer than that. I go into my office and delete the video of me in the room with her. While watching the video, I want to masturbate but I don't have the time. I put on my street clothes and meet her in the billiard room. Luckily, she's still waiting. We agree to go to Ben's Chili Bowl.

Something about this woman makes me want to abandon everything I believe in. I've had one hook-up in my entire life, but I'm willing to do it again tonight if she'll let me. Our conversation has been shallow, so I try to pry information from her but she doesn't bite. I can tell her mind is elsewhere because she keeps checking her phone. I ask her if she's single, and she says that she is. But deep down, I know that she's probably lying.

I try to have a mundane conversation with her, but she's not interested in that either, so I decide that we should part ways. As we walk back to the club from Ben's Chili Bowl, I can't help but study the movement of her hips. The stud in me decides to surface, and I ostentatiously flirt with her. I say, "Earlier you said you wanted to talk about my dance. I can show you the extended version if you like." She becomes giggly and tries to decline my offer, but she eventually takes the bait, gives in, and agrees to go to my condo. She catches me off guard when she asks, "Am I gonna have to pay for my time with you?"

I start laughing hysterically. "What!?"

She stares at me with the most serious look on her face, but I keep laughing, "Oh, you're funny. I strip, but I don't prostitute myself. I'm genuinely attracted to you."

"Sorry if I offended you. You know, maybe we should…"

"No, it's okay. You didn't." I like how cautious she is, letting me know she doesn't do this regularly.

A serious look overcomes her face. "I have another question," she says, and I motion for her to ask.

"Are you a serial killer, rapist, thief, or any other type of criminal? Have you ever been convicted of a crime, including misdemeanors?"

I put on my serious face, but inside I can't help thinking that's she's so cute. "Damn, woman, you're serious, huh? No to all of the above. Are you? Have you?"

She cracks a smile and says, "No. I guess I'll follow you. Just know I'm stronger than I look, and I have a gun."

I'm glad she asked. I presume most people don't think about all of that when they're about to have a one night stand. Which means she probably doesn't do this often. I'm not so sure I want to do this anymore. She could have something.

"We don't have to do this if you're nervous, Robin."

She doesn't change her mind, and I shake my nerves away. The plan is to go to a hotel instead of my condo, but I need to stop at home for a second to pick up my strap, just in case she decides to let me use it. I haven't had sex for almost two years, so if I am going to get it in, I may as well try to go all in.

I tell her I'll meet her at the hotel, but she decides to follow me to my place so she doesn't get lost. *She probably thinks I'll try to ditch her.* Truthfully, I don't know if I would come back out once I made it into the house — my rationality would probably kick in. But we've come this far, so I have to be committed.

As she follows me upstairs, I ask her if she's okay. I feel knots forming in my stomach. I mean, I don't know this woman. I constantly stress to my dancers how unsafe it is for them to go home with club patrons. Granted, most of them are men, but just because Robin is a woman doesn't make her any less crazy. I pause before opening my front door. I'm glad I keep my place clean. I offer her a drink, but she declines. We stand and examine each other's faces for a moment. She asks me if we can take a shower together. I lead the way from my dimly lit living room to my bedroom. I sit on the bed and ask, "Do you go to the doctor regularly?"

To my relief, she says, "Yes, every year."

"Cool, great, great, so do I."

When we are both naked, I take her into the bathroom. I've never had a woman in my place before, and the first time I do it's a random chick from the club. I tell her to get in the shower, and I grab her a washcloth and towel from the linen closet and a toothbrush from under the sink.

"Is this a stripper pole in the shower?"

"Huh?" I say as if I didn't hear the question.

"Is this a stripper pole built into the ceiling?" Through the glass door, I see her look down at the floor then up at the ceiling. "Are those rails on the ceiling? What kind of freaky shit do you get into?"

"It's not what you think," I tell her.

She starts laughing, "You have a stripper pole in the shower that's shooting out water, two rails on the ceiling, and what's this on the floor, some sort of landing pad?"

"I promise I can explain it. I need to practice discretely, so I customized my shower by putting in a stripper pole with small holes for the water, and the rails on the ceiling are so I can practice my flips."

"Who puts a stripper pole in the shower? I must say, it is creative. I was wondering why the shower was so big."

"I took out a room and expanded my bathroom. I tried to make this space function as a small studio and bathroom without it looking too weird."

"So, the rod on the wall over there?"

"It's a beam I stretch on." Before she can ask me too many more questions, I tell her to watch. I climb the pole and position my legs over the bars so I can hang upside down. I tell her to step toward me, and I kiss her upside down. She slides her hands up my torso toward my pussy. I become overly excited and light-headed. I don't want to lose my balance, so I gently push her back and grab the pole. I elongate my body and slink around the pole. When I have a good grip, I swing my lower body down and place my feet on the floor.

I say, "Pick one—dominant or submissive." She looks confused for a second, then she says, "I don't know. Which do you prefer?"

"Dominant or submissive?"

"Submissive."

"Your safe word is 'worm' if you want me to completely stop, if you want me to move on, say 'bird.'"

"Worm?"

"Yeah, it will throw the mood." She tries to change the safe word, but I quiet her by pressing her against the glass shower door. I put her hands above her head and cross her wrists. I tell her I'm not psycho, and I'm not into anything crazy, but she needs to know that I'm in charge. She bites her lip and says okay. I tell her to spread her legs open as I strip her clothes away. When I take mine off I command that she keep her hands above her head.

I grab the liquid soap and drip it down her left shoulder. I bend over and suck her nipple gently before spreading the soap, swiping it across and down her upper torso. I grab her breast and rub the silky cream in a circular motion around her nipples. She moans softly, her tongue caressing the edge of her lips — it's magnetic. I kiss her feverishly. I tell her to spread her legs open. She does, but not enough. I spread them apart even more with my knees. I kiss her from her chin down to the hairs that stop just below her belly button. I bite on her hipbone and caress her ass. I want to eat her pussy right now, but I contain myself.

I stand up and turn her body, so she's now facing the glass wall. I smack her ass and gently wrap my fingers around her neck, then apply a little bit of pressure. I close the gap between us and press my entire body against hers. She sticks her ass out, signaling she wants more. She's too quiet for my liking. I smack her ass repeatedly, each time harder than before. She is still too quiet. I pin her arms behind her back before swiftly, turning her around to face me. I've been playfully restraining her, but there's something in her eyes I can't quite explain. I think she wants more, so I ask if she's ready for me to fuck her.

She breaks her silence. "Only if you really can fuck me good. I'm not your girl, so don't try to make love to me. If you're going to do it, do it."

I command her to get out of the shower. While she's drying off, I go into my bedroom, put on my strap, and crawl into the bed.

"Come here," I say with authority.

When she's standing in front of me, I lean back on my elbows and tell her, "Rub the lube on my dick... Now on your pussy... Play with yourself... Stick your fingers inside you... Deeper. Go deeper, get deeper, Robin." Watching her obey my commands is arousing me in a way that I haven't felt before. If it weren't for this harness, my wetness would be dripping down my leg. Being in control of another person's arousal has always fascinated me, but I've never experienced it outside of fantasizing. I don't know what is driving me to try it with her, but there is no turning back now. I can't let her know, I don't know what I'm doing.

I slide the side of my hand between her breast toward her chin when my hand is positioned so that I can grab her neck, I quickly flip my hand over and palm her throat with a tolerable pressure. Her mouth gapes open. I pinch her nipple. She begins to moan. I slide all the way back to the headboard and tell her to come stand above me in a frisk position. She places both her hands on the wall and I guide her hips toward my tongue. As I eat her pussy, the side of her face is flush with the paint. She grabs a fist full of my hair and thrusts her clit into my mouth. My wig shifts, so I tell her to put her hand back on the wall. I steady my tongue and curve it inside her; she slides her clit back and forth against my taste buds. I feel her pussy swelling, so I pull my tongue away from her.

"Sit on my dick," I tell her.

She moans as she tries to ease the nine inches inside her. I grab her ass and thrust upwards into her. She lets out a screeched mixture of ecstasy and pain. I wait about two seconds to see if she's going to say the safe word. She begins to rise and fall rapidly. "Grab the headboard," I tell her.

Before she can get comfortable, I raise my hips from the bed and fuck her deep. Our pace intensifies. She bounces up and down, and I push into her faster. I see her wetness dripping down the strap, and I push harder. Each time she drops her hips, I pull her into me with greater force. Her screams advance into cursing; I fuck her harder. Sweat glistens on her stomach. She keeps throwing her head back, but I need to see her face. "Look at me, Robin." She doesn't, so I flip her onto the bed and grip her neck. "Look at me, Robin."

She refuses. When I slip out of her, I tell her to get on her knees. I enter her from behind, then push her down so she's lying flat on her stomach. I hold her ass cheeks open as I fuck her pussy. I love watching the strap disappear inside her.

She begins to scream uncontrollably. "Fuck me. Fuck me like you mean it, Katana."

Something barbaric takes over in me when she calls me Katana. I smack her ass, lean down, and wrap my arm around her neck. I am not choking her, but the threat is there. The sound of her moans deepen, her pussy tightens, pushing the dildo out of her, I stop.

We take about half a minute to relax, then I tell her to sit on my face backwards. I gently lick her juices away, following up with soft kisses on her outer lips. When I lay on my back, she positions us in a 69, licks her juices off the dildo, and then sticks her fingers inside of me. I'm on the verge of cumming, and I know that if she keeps hitting my G-spot I am going to squirt. I stop her just before I become unable to stop the explosion. She slides her pussy down my torso and sits on the dick with her back to me. She raises my spread legs in the air and begins to ride me. With one hand, she plunges her fingers in and out of me. With the other hand, she holds my legs steady. We rock into each other. We would be pussy to pussy if the strap weren't there.

She looks over her shoulder at me and says, "Do you want to cum inside me?"

"Fuck yes."

She lets my heels go and puts her elbows and knees on the bed. I raise to my elbows and put the dildo back inside her. She bucks backward into me as I thrust into her. We begin to curse and lose ourselves to our own rhythms. I cum just before she does, then she lets all her frustration go, burying her screams in the mattress. Her grind slows, and I relax. Eventually, we separate and fall fast asleep on separate corners of the bed. We sleep for about two hours, then she taps me on my shoulder. She is trying to wake me, but I've been awake since she crawled out of the bed. I've always been a light sleeper. I was worried that she might go through my things, but she didn't, she found her clothes and showered.

She whispers, "Katana, I have to go to work."

I roll over and stretch, "Call me Camille."

"Camille?"

"It's my government name." Shock briefly crosses her face, but she doesn't say anything.

"Do you want to get breakfast?"

"No I'm fine, thank you for last night."

"That's not necessary."

She pats my leg and tells me she is gonna go. I anxiously get out of the bed and stand. The left corner of her mouth flinches upward, but she quickly flattens out her smile. I'm still naked. She eyes me up and down and then looks at the floor. I go over and hug her.

While we say our goodbyes, she says, "Maybe we can do this again sometime."

"Sounds like a plan to me." She kisses me on my cheek and whispers, "Check your pocket," then trots away.

I pull out a folded piece of paper. I smile and yell, "I already have your number!"

She turns around. "I know, but now you have my personal one." I watch her get into her car and then go back to my condo to clean up.

I pick up the sheets and find a diamond ring. The rock looks to be about three karats. I slide the ring onto my pinky finger. She must've hidden this in her pocket.

3

NADIA
April 7th, 2011

Usually, the drive down the Baltimore-Washington Parkway gives me a chance to clear my head, but right now, that's not the case. I've pulled into a gas station parking lot because the rain is too thick to drive through.

Through the veil on my windshield, I see two homeless women making their way under a bridge. Watching them distracts me from the list of questions I writing down for Laila. I don't want to forget anything during our confrontation. My mind tends to go blank when I'm angry.

The women under the bridge remind me of a time in my life when I was homeless and scrambling for shelter. Even though my life has changed drastically, I try not to think about that time in my life because I feel like I did it to myself. For a while, I tried to blame everything on my ex-husband, but eventually, I had to acknowledge that I was being selfish when I came out to him.

Maybe this shit with Laila is what I deserve. If I didn't believe it before, I believe it now — karma is a motherfucker.

The rain begins to let up, so I hurriedly finish writing my questions and get back on the road toward Laila's house.

As I get closer, I turn my radio up and blast "Rollin' in the Deep." I fly around the corner into her cul-de-sac at forty miles per hour and angrily pull into her driveway. I down the rest of my Red Bull and scream, "We could have had it all," as I screech to a halt. I slam my car door and stomp to the front door. I bang my fist on it repeatedly, kick it once, and wait with my arms crossed.

When it opens, a huge belly protruding from a muscle shirt stuns me.

The pregnant woman looks at the sheet of paper in my hand. "Are you a reporter? Because Laila isn't here."

"No, I'm... I'm—"

She interrupts my stumbling. "Wait? Are you one of the bitches I saw on TV yesterday? Get the fuck away from here." She slams the door in my face before I can respond.

My stomach bunches and ties around itself. I lean closer to the door and yell, "My name is Nadia." She doesn't open it. I yell again. "Tori, we need to talk." I use her nickname to exert friendliness.

"You're the one who sent the pantsuit, aren't you?!" she says while opening the door. I suddenly realize that she is the primary woman in Laila's life.

I lose my confidence and say, "This is inappropriate. I'm gonna go."

"Nope. You brought your ass over here, so let's talk."

Again, I try to explain how inappropriate it is that I've come, here but she cuts me off.

"Inappropriate! Shit, you crossed the line when you stepped on the porch."

I try to explain my actions. "I wasn't expecting you to be here."

"Why not? I fucking live here!" she says matter-of-factly.

"Laila said you were out of town."

She's quiet for a moment, then she rolls her eyes and steps to the side.

"Come in."

A red flag goes up. "That's okay. I'm gonna go."

"I'm seven—almost eight months pregnant. What am I gonna do?" She has a point, so I follow her in.

Things are as I remember them, except for the yellow, red, and green baby items scattered everywhere. I feel deeply uncomfortable.

"Do you want something to drink, Nadia?"

Her politeness throws me off. I wave my hand back and forth. "Look, we can stop with the pleasantries. We know what this is."

"Tell me what *it* is," she says while making herself comfortable in the armchair.

"Listen, Victoria. I had no idea you two were still together. She told me you left and moved to Wisconsin."

She rubs her hands across her lap. "I went to visit, but that's beside the point. You knew about me."

Sarcastically I say, "I know you left her."

Her lips get tight. "When did you meet her?"

I know the exact day I met Laila, but I give an ambiguous answer. "October? November-ish?"

"How much did y'all fuck?"

Victoria's question stuns me. I don't know what to say, "Whoa, what?"

I cross my arms in front of my chest. She asks me to have a seat because I'm making her nervous.

As soon as I sit, she asks, "Did y'all have a threesome with that other chick?"

"No! Hell no. I met her and we dated for months before we had sex. I love her—"

She tries to talk over me, spurting out, "You love her! Ha."

"Don't degrade my relationship."

"Your relationship? News flash, Nadia. She's taken."

"Yep, by me! You left her, went and got pregnant, and now she's moved on."

Victoria yells, "You don't know what the fuck you're talking about!"

"Well, she told me you're a non-factor."

"News alert, Nadia! We're getting married, so that makes you a non-factor."

I laugh. "Victoria, she has a girlfriend outside of you. Do you really think she wants you?"

"And what makes you think she wants *you*? Because she was double-timing you, too."

I pause because she's right but quickly bark back, "That other chick saved her life, Victoria. She's not with her."

"Saved her life? You must not have seen what I saw."

"Whatever. This is bullshit I'm done tal—"

"Ow. Ow. Owww!" A strained scream supplemented by short breaths interrupts my sentence.

I reach for her. "Are you all right?"

She puts up her hand, motioning for me to keep away.

Tori breaks into a sweat, stretches her legs out, and struggles to say, "Call an ambulance. Something is wrong."

Internally, I panic. *Okay, okay. Umm, pull it together, Nadia. What are you gonna do?* "Let me take you," I tell Victoria. "It'll be faster. Where's your purse or wallet or whatever?" I say frantically while skimming the room.

She grunts while leaning back on the couch. "On the table at the top of the stairs."

I run up the stairs and grab the wallet from a table beneath a portrait of *my woman* and her woman embracing each other. I roll my eyes.

*

Victoria groans again as I get her strapped into the car. I try to ease her mind by grabbing her hand and stroking it with my thumb. "Try to stay calm. We'll be at the hospital soon. How far along are you?"

"Almost eight months!"

"You did say that. You're *so* tiny."

"I'm high-risk."

"I understand. I was too."

We fall silent, except for Victoria's painful cries.

It takes about forty minutes to get Victoria from the emergency room to the labor and delivery floor. I've tried to leave numerous times, but she won't let me, and I keep obliging her because I think our argument pushed her into labor.

In the room, Tori's contractions slow and she asks me to be honest with her about Laila. I try to end the conversation before it gets started, but she doesn't take the hint, saying, "No, go ahead. I want to hear what makes you special."

I scoff. "Makes me special? What do you mean?"

She tries to sit up on the bed, but she's unable to reposition herself without pain. I step toward her. She puts her hand up and says, "Tell me what y'all did together!"

"You mean, like, activities?"

"That works."

"Bowling, museums, poetry shows, pottery, strip clubs."

Tori huffs as if I'm lying. "Laila doesn't do strip clubs!"

"Laila bought me my first lap dance. One time we went to this bar and rode the mechanical bull, which she's pretty good at." I fake a laugh because this feels wrong to push her buttons this way but I can't let her best me. I can't let her know how humiliated I feel. "If you could've seen her bouncing up and down."

Tori frowns, but fuck it. I hope it hurts. I know I'm wrong for redirecting my anger towards her, but it feels good to make someone else feel the pain I do.

Victoria barks, "Shut up."

"Well, don't ask questions you don't want the answer to."

"What makes you think you're in love with my woman?"

In my head, the reasons rapidly surface.

I love her because we connected on so many different levels. She brings out the best in me more often than the worst. When I'm with her, it feels like I'm the only person on this earth who matters. I don't have to think about what will make her happy, it's natural. Simply, it feels good when I'm with her. I believe she's my soulmate.

"Nadia, tell me why you think you love her."

She breaks my thoughts, so I respond angrily. "Because she loves me in a way I've never felt before. She touches my libido until I expel every little piece of my DNA into her mouth, onto her hands, even onto her cunt sometimes--"

She turns apple red. "Bitch, get the fuck out!"

I grin. Suddenly, the door to the room clicks open. I scramble to a chair in the corner like a misbehaving child. Laila's voice creeps around the door. I jump back to my feet before my ass is fully on the cushion. Fear, sadness, and guilt overwhelm me. The reality that I will never have Laila the way I want crushes me. I fight to hold back my tears.

Victoria says, "Laila, listen," and reveals my presence by pointing in my direction. The look on Laila's face is priceless. She tries to talk to me, but I dismiss myself from the room.

I run to the elevator and repeatedly push the down button. As the elevator door closes behind me, tears begin to fall. Laila reopens the doors by sticking her perfectly manicured hand inside. She steps onto the elevator and apologizes about five times before I say anything. The self-restraint I'm exhibiting ought to win me a goddamn Oscar.

Laila brings me out of silently staring at her when she tries to schedule a meeting for us to chat about what's going on. I lose it.

"Are you fucking serious right now? A meeting?"

"Nadia, I'm sorry."

"You're sorry about what? Being a fucking liar?"

"About things exploding this way."

"Oh, so you're sorry you got caught. Not for stringing me along or making me look like a fucking fool on TV. On national fucking TV. I want to beat the shit out of you right now."

She reaches for me. I scream, "Don't fucking touch me. I hate you."

"Nadia, I'm sorry."

"Go back and be with your baby momma, who you told me left you, by the way."

"She did, but she came back and--"

"And you wanted to have your cake and eat it too. Get the fuck outta here."

"It wasn't like that. I didn't expect any of this."

"And now that it's here—now what?" I don't give her a chance to respond. "The thing is, Laila, you shouldn't be apologizing right now because all of this was in your control. If you weren't a cheating son of a—" The elevator doors open and a woman eyes us for a second before looking down at her phone, opting to take the next elevator. I lower my voice. "If you weren't a cheater, none of this would be happening."

"Nadia, calm down and listen, please."

"Don't tell me what the fuck to do."

"Nadia!"

"No... You know what? I will calm down because I'm done with your trifling ass."

When the elevator doors open to the first floor, I tell her *goodbye* in the most patronizing way I can, push the button for the seventh floor, and walk away with my middle finger extended behind my back.

As I'm walking to my car, I wonder why I was talking to Victoria like she was my best friend. In the back of my mind, I knew something was still up between them, but I chose to ignore it. In the car, I grip the steering wheel and laugh out a spit bubble while thinking: *The woman I love is not only engaged to another woman, but also in love with a third. She has three lovers that I know of, and I don't know where I fall on the pyramid. Laila Morriston is a master of deception. I don't know what was and wasn't true in our relationship.*

When I asked Laila to be my girlfriend, she knew she was involved with other women. She didn't have to say yes. I don't understand how you can screw so many people over and act like everything is okay. She knew from the very beginning that I was attracted to her, but that I would have been fine only being her friend. I feel like I am going to have a panic attack so I get out the car and start pacing around it. I kick my tire and throw my body across the hood. I hear a child ask, "Is that lady alright, so we check on her?" I stand up, wipe the tears away, get back into the car, and tell myself that everything is going to be okay.

4

NADIA cont'd

I don't want to be alone, so I go to my boss's house. Rosa, the house assistant, is walking down the corridor when I open the door. I ask her where Mrs. Spady is and request she make me a rum and Coke. I find Mrs. Spady watching a soap opera in the yoga room. She says, "Hi my love without looking at me."

"Hi."

I'm silently standing in the doorway looking at Mrs. Spady when Rosa brings me the drink. I play with it for a few minutes then burst into tears, catching both of them off guard. Mrs. Spady turns her head toward me, "What's wrong baby girl?"

"My life is a soap opera," I belt out.

Mrs. Spady says, "Ahh. This is about Laila. I knew you'd let it out eventually."

"I'm in love with her, and she's getting married."

"Dia, I know you want that fish, but you should ask yourself—why her?"

"Because... because..."

She shushes me. "I don't need to know why. I already know. You need to evaluate that for yourself."

"How do you already know?"

"Baby, I've been there."

I switch to calling her ma'am so she won't think I'm being disrespectful. "Ma'am, have you ever been humiliated on TV?"

She maneuvers her seventy-year-old frame into an upright position and summons me to the couch by patting it. I sit down, and she hugs me. "Don't cry, baby girl. It's going to be okay! At some point or another, everyone experiences what you're going through. It may present itself differently, but at the end of the day, the heartbreak is the same."

"What did you do to get through it?"

"I wrote a book."

I breathe out a laugh. "*A book?!*"

"Yes."

I lift my head from her bosom. "Like, a *book book*?"

"Well, more like a journal. I wrote my thoughts down so they wouldn't be running through my head, and it turned into a book."

My tears begin to dry up. She pats my leg, "Go to the library and look on the third shelf of the fifth column, grab the blue book with gold letters, and spend some quality time with it."

"Now?" I ask.

"Yes! Go before my program comes back from commercial. And, along the way, tell Alex to make jambalaya for dinner."

She declines my offer to come back and sit with her, and I am totally okay with that because the news is about to come on, and honestly, I don't want to see a bunch of depressing shit anyway. Living it is enough.

I retrieve the book from the library and go sit outside on the patio. The book has part two imprinted on the spine in small caps. I open it, and every page is blank. For a second, I'm baffled. Then it dawns on me—she's encouraging me to write down my feelings.

Dear Purple Book: I didn't envision my first lesbian experience like this. For some reason, I thought it would be easier dating women, but the cloak of naïvety got me again. I finally decided to take a leap and let myself be attracted to someone, and I got a plate full of bullshit.

I'm so angry for not being more cautious. Maybe I should have given one of the women Mrs. Spady tried to hook me up with a chance. Then maybe I wouldn't be reconsidering my life. I came out four years ago, and after being humiliated on national television, I think I want to go back in the closet.

From the moment I met Laila, I took her to be an extremely honest person. I never would've thought she'd fuck me over in such an epic way. She played me like a fool. No, she played me ingeniously; I acted foolishly. When I saw her that first time I thought I would regret it if I didn't say hello. The irony is; I am regretting that hello now.

I asked that bitch repeatedly if she was available and ready to move on, and each time she told me yes. God, why am I so naïve? Every time I decide to let my guard down and open my heart to people, things get fucked up. It didn't work with men, and now this situation is making me think it's not worth it being with women. Every time I face my sexuality, I get burned. Maybe this is a sign.

* * *

The morning sunshine startles me awake. I don't know what time I fell asleep. When I turn over to look at the time the journal pokes me in the side. *I must've fallen asleep while writing.* It's 9:03. I lay on the edge of the bed and reflect on everything that happened yesterday. Victoria and the baby are plaguing my thoughts.

My curiosity has gotten the best of me, and so here I am in the hospital gift shop buying a balloon and a teddy bear. When I get to the seventh floor, I inch Victoria's room door open without knocking. I peep around the corner and excitedly say congratulations. Laila is standing with her back to the door, looking out the window. A guy is sitting on the sofa next to her. Laila quickly turns around with an evil look on her face. The first thing I notice is that her eyes are red. The man looks at me strangely and then stands.

"Leave!" Laila says without the usual *please* she uses when making a demand. I look at the hospital bed for confirmation of Laila's decision, as if Victoria and I are cool somehow. Victoria's face is blank like she's in shock. The man starts walking toward me. I creep backward out the door.

I am wronger than wrong in this situation. How fucked up am I to ruin a moment that's supposed to be filled with happiness?

No matter my intention, I can feel that something is wrong here, which makes my presence even more awful.

The man follows me out of the room and asks who I am. I'm about to ask him what right he has to question me, but he hasn't done anything for me to pop off on him. After I tell him my name, he tells me that he's Trey, Laila's best friend, who I knew nothing about.

Reality keeps slapping me in the face. As much as I thought I was Laila's girlfriend, it's becoming clearer that I don't know shit about this woman.

Trey says, "Look, I know we don't know each other, so don't take this the wrong way, but it would be best if you left Laila and Victoria alone. They're going through some tough shit—"

I put my hand up. "Hold up! Wait one damn minute. Are you the break-up crew? How dare you tell me what to do."

"Let me stop you right there, Miss Lady. We need to go outside or to the lobby. You're not going to do this today. I came at you civilly and Trey is not the one."

"Yeah, let's do that."

Outside, Trey says, "I know you're hurt, but the sooner you get over her, the better."

"She needs to tell me that herself."

"I've known her for twelve years, and I know she loves Tori and wants to be with her—"

"She—" I try to talk, but he cuts me off.

"I *know* how you feel because my lover cheated on me. But, at the end of the day, familiarity will always trump fun."

"Fun?" I get pistol hot and walk off so I don't bitch slap his ass.

He yells, "Hey!" But I take off running.

Tears and snot are running rampant by the time I reach the car. Trey's words play on repeat in my mind, tormenting me: *Familiarity will always trump fun.* In other words, I was just the fun girl until Laila had a chance to work it out with Tori.

I drive aimlessly for two hours then decide to go home to my dog.

When I open the door to my condominium, Bruno's eighty-pound self-tackles me. I haven't seen him in a couple of days because I've been staying with Mrs. Spady.

I find a note from the dog walker, saying she came by more often after realizing I hadn't been home and she'll bill me accordingly. I ball up the note and put it in the trash. When I look down into the bin, I see a cigar wrapper. I get excited, walk to the bedroom, and retrieve the joint Laila and I didn't finish.

I light it, fall back onto the bed, and remember the first time Laila and I smoked. We went to a comedy show at DC Improv and left giggly as hell. That's when we made love for the first time.

Laila was like, "Man, I wish I had some weed," and it just so happens—Mrs. Spady uses it for her arthritis and I'm the one who picks it up.

I remember the way Laila pulled my hair back and elongated my neck, and how she gently wrapped her lips and teeth around the area just below my ear. We were playfully wrestling on the bed in my room when she ended up behind me. We were on our knees and I kept bucking my hips into her trying to get away, but she wouldn't let me and then she pulled my earlobe between her lips and put her left hand on my waist. My wetness was out of control. I tried to turn around to kiss her, but she restrained me. She bit the back of my neck, and I bucked my hips into her pelvis as I fell forward.

Thinking about how Laila placed delicate kisses all over my upper back and how she pinned my wrists to my lower back has me dripping wet—my pussy is throbbing. I put the joint down and scramble out of my panties on the way to my bedroom. I crawl into the bed, lie on my stomach, and rub my clit.

The way she made me feel was out of this world. I didn't know that I could enjoy being bitten and contorted so much. I sure as hell never thought that someone grinding on my ass would drive me to an orgasm. I loved how aggressive she was. Everything blew my mind from the warmth and softness of her pubes to the way she placed her hands between my shoulder blades and slowly began to grind on my ass.

I bucked my hips upwards, trying to match her rhythm, and rubbed my clit furiously. Her panting picked up and she increased the pressure of her grind. She whispered, "Nadia, I'm gonna cum."

I begged, "Let me feel you."

She said, "Oh, fuck," then abruptly lifted away from me. I turned onto my side to look at her. I couldn't tell if she came or if something else was wrong. She lay on the bed and instructed me to taste her while ushering me towards her pussy. Trying not to show my confusion, I hopped on my knees and placed my tongue on her.

All I could do was obey, and I obeyed by pushing her legs to the ceiling and sticking my tongue deep inside her. When she was close to cumming again, she stopped me by lifting my chin.

She rolled me onto my back, and I didn't know what she was doing, but it felt amazing. She was kind of curling her tongue onto itself and then unrolling it inside of me. I remember never wanting her to stop. She didn't touch my clit at all, and I was about to explode furiously. When she opened her eyes and looked at me, my eyes locked with hers. My heart said *I love her*, and she winked at me. Next, she positioned herself in a way that I was not ready for emotionally or physically.

She said, "I want you to feel something. Spread your legs as wide open as you can."

I did and she sat in between them. For the first time, I felt how amazing it was being pussy to pussy. Her wetness began to fill me as mine fought upwards into her. The slickness of her juices, the warmth I felt when she was on my ass—they were nothing compared to this. In that moment, we were making love. Until then, I had never had an orgasm that left me utterly exhausted. I felt like I'd graduated to the next level of lesbianism. But now, I'm all fucked up because my lover/teacher has abandoned me.

My climax is full of frustration. I pull my hand from between my legs and sit up. I need to take a break from her, from all of this. Maybe Trey is right. I need to move on and fast.

Damn, she really is a good fuck, though. Oh, my god. I was just a fuck to her — that makes sense. I mean, I barely know anything about her. It was just sex, sex, sex. I light the joint again and take another puff. While blowing the smoke out, I admit to myself that I was a goddamn jump off. That motherfuckin' Laila played me like a fucking harp. Just as beautifully and gracefully as she wanted to. Oh, fuck that. It's about to go down.

Bruno starts whining, and I turn my head toward the door. He drops down on his front paws and starts making a high-pitched whimper, signaling he needs to pee. I stamp out the joint, put on my running clothes, and take him on a jog. My mind is reeling with possibilities for how I'm going to handle this bitch.

*

Thirty minutes later, when Bruno and I arrive back home, there are two messages on my voicemail. I don't recognize the number, but it's not an option to ignore calls because it could be for Mrs. Spady.

The first message is from Laila. She says, "Nadia, sorry is not enough in this situation, but I must apologize. I need to see you. I don't want you to be mad at me forever. I want to see you again. I owe you a face-to-face. Call me back, please."

The second one is also from Laila, "Nadia, please don't ignore me. What we have is real—" She's cut off by a male voice. "Laila, I know you're not calling other women on my phone! Victoria is in there crying over your stillborn, and you're out here—"

The message cuts off.

Stillborn? I listen to the message again. Xavier and I got pregnant in our second year of marriage, but the baby was stillborn because his liver didn't develop properly. We decided not to try again and the next year adopted Olivia when she was three. Losing a baby is too much to cope with, and I went to the hospital today like a fucking moron. I definitely need to remove myself from this situation.

5

TORI
April 15, 2011

"It's time to discharge you, Ms. Greer." As soon as I look at Nurse Neal, my anxiety level spikes.

"I don't know if I'm ready."

The nurse sits on the bed with me. "I know, ladybug. The next couple of weeks are going to be hard, but you're gonna make it."

"I don't know if I should." I start mumbling through sobs. "I killed my baby."

"Oh, don't think like that. These things happen. It just wasn't time." In a motherly way, the nurse places her hand on my back. "Look, I put a journal in this bag so you can write down your feelings. And I included some information about grief."

"Do you think I'll be okay?"

"I do. It's gonna be tough because losing a baby is one of the hardest things one can go through, but I do think you will be okay."

Laila comes into the room, cutting our conversation short. I say thank you and goodbye to Nurse Neal and leave the hospital.

"We're gonna be okay, right Laila?"

Laila nods at me convincingly, but her face reads scared to death.

*

The outside of the house looks gray. It's been raining the past few days, and it's finally stopped, but the clouds still haven't parted enough to let the afternoon sunshine through. I don't want to go into the house because... *because life isn't fucking fair and I fucked up and I don't want to be faced with the sadness of what I've done.* I feel gray.

A soft thud pulls my attention away from the neighbors entering their front door. I didn't notice Trey standing in our driveway. He's bearing his weight down on the trunk to make sure it is secured. He steadies his feet on the ground and turns in our direction.

I lightly press on the brakes and bring the car to a stop. Laila sent him to the house hours ago to remove all the baby stuff. She doesn't think I heard her on the phone, telling him to do it but I did. I pay attention to everything she does. She doesn't think I pay attention anymore, but I do. I've just been... *been so caught up in my own shit, dealing with my own grief, that I've neglected to be there for her the way I need to.* I've been trying to figure out how I could have prevented our baby from dying.

I'm not sure I'm completely on board with removing everything so quickly, but I didn't put up a fight. And besides, there was no reason to argue about it because her reasoning was logical: As time goes on, it will be harder to let it go. In any event, Trey was supposed to be gone by now. He looks at us for a moment then gets into his car.

I look over at Laila in the passenger seat. She's gently brushing away the tear that just landed on her jeans, trying to keep it from soaking into the denim. I ask, "Do you want him to stay?" She shakes her head no.

I stick my hand out of the window and yell for him to back out of the driveway. I immediately regret yelling because my throat still hurts from the intubation. They had to intubate me and do an emergency C-section because I had Vasa Previa. They said that was the official cause of the baby bleeding out, but I know it's because of what I did.

Trey pulls up and gives us a smile that doesn't do anything to distract from the look of sympathy in his eyes. He doesn't say anything. Laila leans forward and talks past me, "Thanks, Trey. I'll call you in a few."

My instinct is to say, *In a few what? In a few minutes, days, hours?* It irks my nerves that Laila is never specific about anything, but I don't want to be mean. I can't be mean because I know she's hurting too. *I killed our baby.*

Trey says to Laila, "Okay. Talk to you soon," but he's looking into my eyes. I give him a quick forced smile and then look down because I'm ashamed. He knows what I've done.

When Laila and I walk into the house, I see why it took him so long to leave. He has snatched up all the baby stuff and returned the photos of me and Laila to their respective places. At some point during all of our fighting, we packed them up. My eyes are drawn beyond the back of the Lazy Boy chair to the curved vacuum lines on the floor. An hour or so ago, a blue and yellow playpen with a matching swing filled the now empty space. I drop my bags and walk over to the space that was converted from a home gym into a playroom.

Laila tries to comfort me. "Baby, we will get through this together. I promise."

"That's hard to believe."

"I mean, things will be rough at times, but we will make it together."

My chest hurts. The weight of not having him here brings me to my knees. I want to scream, but only tears and gasps come out.

"I can't deal with this pain, Laila. I feel like there is no recovering. How can I live with what I've done and it doesn't matter that I was raped, I shouldn't have taken that abortion pill."

Laila sits on the floor in front of me and strokes my hands with her thumbs. "Shh, shh. Tori, you can't blame yourself. This wasn't your fault, okay?"

I thrust backward and collapse onto the floor, wanting to fall through it. I curl in my lips and try to stop the flood of tears.

"Laila, I need some time alone," I say. "I'm not trying to be mean or anything. I just need time to... to—"

"I understand. Just know that I am here for you. Whatever you need, just say it. I won't be too far away."

"Thank you."

6

LAILA
May 21, 2011

The clouds have brought us rain this morning. I didn't sleep much last night because I kept checking on Tori. I probably should have taken one of her sleeping pills, but I needed to think.

Everything in our life is upside-down right now. In three months, it will be September, one year since Tori's rape, and they still haven't caught the guy. One year since I made the decision to get involved with two unsuspecting women, and one year since I abandoned my morals.

At that time, I didn't realize how hurt I still felt about Tori cheating on me. I truly thought I had forgiven her, but I was only stuffing it down. I haven't trusted her since the first time it happened. Every time her actions changed, her cheating was the first place my mind went. If she stayed at work late, tried to go someplace alone, didn't return my calls fast enough, I thought she was out with another woman. I stopped having loving thoughts of her. They were overshadowed by resentment. And she constantly tried to redeem herself, but it wasn't enough. It was never going to be enough. Being stuck on what I thought she was doing caused me to miss the signs. I was so jaded that I mistook signs of trauma as proof she had been unfaithful.

Revenge became my driving force and, like the Buddha said, "Holding on to anger is like grasping a hot coal with the intent of throwing it at someone else; you are the one who gets burned."

Now I have to undo my mess.

7

CAMILLE

Secretly, I was hoping that I would run into Laila here, but I didn't fully prepare for it. I park next to her car and wait for her to exit the nursing home. From a distance, I see her looking down at her cell phone. I hop out of the truck, open the tailgate, and casually sit there swinging my legs. When she notices me, I wave at her indifferently. She starts smacking the phone against her leg nervously but doesn't break her stride.

Laila opens the passenger door on her BMW, throws her purse in, then greets me at the truck. I hop down, and she says, "Pick me up." I pick up her small frame and place her on the tailgate. I opt to stand, so I can rock back and forth. It's a nervous tick I have.

"My parents have been calling me," I tell her. Laila looks baffled. "You've unknowingly awakened Goliath."

"Sorry," she says.

I roll my eyes at her and stick my hands in my pockets, "But are you really? I haven't talked to my parents in five years, and now they're determined to invade my life."

"Camille, I'm sorry. I didn't know. I didn't mean to hurt you or cause you any trouble."

I try to keep my hand gestures contained but cant. I start pointing and waving my finger at her aggressively. "But that the thing you did. You were very careless, Laila. Everything is all fucked up now. I worked so hard to build my little bubble, and being involved with you has threatened that."

"I know, and I'm extremely sorry. There aren't enough words."

"You're damn right, there aren't."

"I need you to explain yourself."

She reaches for my hand. I let her grasp it. "Cam, we both know that any answer I give you will just be an excuse, and I don't want to do that anymore."

I yank my hand from her and throw my hands into the air. "Do what? Ease my mind?"

"Offer excuses. Hurt you anymore."

I look for her eyes, but she's looking down pitifully. I soften my tone. "Laila, you look exhausted."

"Haven't been sleeping much with everything going on." I look at her for a couple of seconds then decide to be compassionate and give her a hug. Being nasty to her isn't going to change anything; the damage has already been done.

"Listen, Laila, on some real kosher-level shit, why don't you come back to my place so I can make you some tea? That always makes you feel better." A tear falls from her eye, and she nods her head in agreement. I go grab her purse and lock up her car.

When I get into the truck with her, she says, "Thank you, Camille."

"NP." That raises a chuckle out of her—she doesn't get why I'm always using abbreviations.

"Camille, what I did was 100 percent fucked up. I was being selfish. I was lonely and I was hurt and I wanted—I needed—to feel something different. The way things unfolded with you and Nadia, and the way things fell apart with Tori... It all happened so fast. And, no offense, I'm just trying to be honest— you were supposed to be a one-night stand, and that's the way it was. But then you showed up at Expected Architecture and even though I didn't realize it at the time, I was hooked on you. You blew my mind, and I wanted you all the time. I thought I could contain our relationship to sex, but you're such an amazing person. I mean, how could I not love you? We have such deep conversations. We're raw with each other, ya know, and I needed that in my life, and I know you may not forgive me for bringing you into this mess, but... well, let me try to explain it."

I sigh and start staring at the clouds. I can't look her in the face while she rehashes what was supposed to be a relationship.

"Things became so convoluted between me and Tori. We were at the point of just co-existing in the same space. Things weren't bad, but we haven't been the same since she cheated on me that last time. I did forgive her, but everything was tainted, ya know. Deep down, deep deep down, I was disgusted with her. I didn't trust her the way I used to, and maybe it wasn't fair to either of us to stay together, but that's what we chose and so we were dealing with it."

I pull a tissue out of the console and hand it to her. "I totally get where you're coming from, Laila, and I'm not holding it against you, but you were in control of what happened. You chose to not be truthful."

"You're right. I just didn't know how to walk it back. I mean, you had to know that something else was going on, right?"

"Truthfully, yeah. Did I want to acknowledge it? No. I knew it wouldn't last, though. I mean, I met you in a strip club. But I didn't expect for you to be with three other people, either."

"Three other people?"

"Tori, Nadia, and Tasha."

"I wasn't with Tasha. She was an intern gone mad. I promise that on everything. I've never been with Tasha. She was on some fatal attraction shit, but without the sex."

"So you never led her on or anything."

"No. I may have been too open with her about my private life, but that was it."

I park in front of my building, and a valet comes to park the car.

Laila says, "Oh, wow."

"That's right, you haven't been to my new place."

"No."

"Well, welcome to Shavano Chateau. They actually have a dance studio, even though I don't dance anymore."

On the elevator, Laila makes it a point to stand far away from me. I tried to stand close to her but she rebuffs it by moving to the other side of the elevator. She looks at me sincerely and says, "Earlier you said that we wouldn't have gone anywhere because we met in a strip club."

"Yeah, we met at a strip club, and you really couldn't get past that."

"I'm gonna have to disagree."

I scoff at her and shake my head. "It showed in the way you treated me. You never saw my true worth. You pigeon-holed me from the beginning, even after I shared my goals with you."

Laila unfolds her arms and tries to assert her innocence. "That's not true. I never judged you."

"Well, that's how you made me feel. You never took the time to find out what makes me tick. To find out my story."

"I was trying to keep it superficial with you."

"Damn. That hurt, Laila."

The elevator door opens, and I exit first. In the apartment, Laila starts apologizing, "I wasn't trying to be mean. You're right, I did put you in a box, but not because you stripped. I wasn't in a good place."

"I believe that, but it was also because, as a stripper, I was beneath you."

Laila sucks her teeth and looks down. I was going to give her a tour, but I decide against it.

"Have a seat, Laila, while I make the tea."

"I'll come to the kitchen with you," she says.

I shrug my shoulders.

"Camille, you're right. When we met, I wasn't gonna give you the time of day. I thought that... maybe, at the most, you could be a booty call, and —"

"Then you found out I have the brains to intern at one of the most prestigious architecture firms in the nation."

"Yeah, and that you're amazing outside of the bedroom, too."

"Do you know that I own the strip club?"

Laila's eyes get big. "Do you know that I own three strip clubs, and I was working inside that one because we were having problems with the liquor license. Do you know that my family disowned me and I hastily married B.J's father. I know you don't because you never inquired about things outside of what I could do with my tongue and fingers. And the small talk you found so interesting was only to move us toward sex or to wrap sex up. And you're right—I knew something was up, but I was having fun with you as well, so I played ignorant. So, in a sense, I guess we used each other. I hadn't had sex in two years, so I was a little backed up."

I hand her a cup of tea, she leans on the counter top and the cup around anxiously.

Laila asks, "So, that means you don't love me."

I swallow hard to ease the hurt in my throat. "That means I don't love you."

She stands and looks around. "Where's the bathroom?"

"Down the hall, take a left. Second door on the right."

When she leaves, I break down momentarily and then quickly pull myself together. I put two sugar cubes in her tea and half a mint leaf. Out loud I say, "Keep it together, Camille. This is almost over. You said what you needed to say to end this."

Laila returns from the bathroom with a tissue in her hand.

"I've dressed your tea for you."

"Thanks," she says.

We sit silently for a while, trying to avoid eye contact, but also trying to be present in the moment.

"Love is a tricky thing, isn't it, Camille?"

"Tell me about it."

"Love is one of those things you can't quantify, predict, reject, or understand. It can mess you up, change your life for the better, make you foolish." Laila pushes away and then pulls the cup of tea back toward her. "I'll probably never admit this again to anymore, but I was in love with three people at once."

"Not possible."

"But it is. My love for each of you didn't grow the same, but I did come to love you all."

"But you weren't truly yourself with all of us."

"I was who I was in those moments. Whatever you all needed me to be, I gave you that."

"Which was still only a portion of you."

"No one gives all of themselves to another all the time."

"True, but you lied time after time after time, and for me, that's not love."

"I'm sorry about that, but I do love all of you."

"How is that possible?"

"In the same way that parents are capable of loving their children equally."

"Hmm... Well, that's bullshit. I think you want to justify your actions by blaming it on love. And for me, love doesn't involve deception."

"That wasn't my intent. I didn't mean for this to happen. I met some beautiful people during a vulnerable time in my life, and then shit got crazy."

"You let shit get crazy."

She drinks the rest of her tea.

"Look, Laila, we can't change anything that happened, so I just want to let you know that I'm gonna be okay. And, to make this easier for you, I don't want to be involved with you anymore. During the last eight months, you told me four times that you want to end this thing, and we both discarded that after a few days. But after this last set of events, I'm calling it quits. I'm not gonna jeopardize my emotional well-being for someone who is... someone who's in love with three people."

Laila sticks her hand out to shake mine. I grip it so she can't pull it away. "Do you have something you want to say?"

"I'm sorry, and be happy."

Laila gathers her things and heads for the door. I prepare to take her back to the nursing home, but she opts to take a cab. When the door closes behind her I try to bury my emotions away by frantically cleaning the house.

In my gut, I knew something was wrong, but I ignored those feelings because I wanted to give my love away and get my rocks off. Where I messed up was that I underestimated the gravity of what a broken heart feels like.

8

NADIA
June 23, 2011

After moping around for two weeks, Mrs. Spady told me to take some time off, so I've come to Pennsylvania to visit Olivia. I didn't realize how much I missed seeing her every day. She's almost nine and needs me more than ever; maybe I need her just as much to keep me grounded.

I know our divorce has affected her deeply because the sparkle in her eyes has faded. We tried to hide things from her as best we could—then I disappeared from her life. I don't know if she will ever understand that leaving her is something I never wanted to do, but my cards were dealt that way. Consequently, these years apart have greatly strained our relationship. For instance, she never calls me Mom, she just starts talking, or when she has something to say, she waits until we make eye contact before speaking. It's almost like she wants to make sure she has my full attention so she doesn't have to say it.

When I asked her about it yesterday, she shrugged her shoulders, so I pressed her. I wasn't ready for what she said. Apparently, her father gets mad every time her grandmother refers to me as her mother or asks if Olivia has talked to me. I need to find a better way to make our new family dynamic work.

I've been here four days and Xavier and I have yet to spend time with Olivia, together. Either he has had her or I have, so today, to show Olivia some solidarity between Xavier and myself, I've set up a lunch date for the three of us, but shit is going haywire. Xavier is tense and has been from the moment he walked through the door. I've asked him to lighten up, but he hasn't and is being snippy. After four years, he's still upset with me, and because of the situation with Laila, I fully understand his sentiments. He feels betrayed.

He says, "This is a waste of time. I don't want to be in your presence. I thought I did, that we could be amicable, but I get pissed when I see you."

"That's funny because, with the way you've been blowing my phone up, you'd think seeing me was your number one priority."

"Look, I only came to tell you face-to-face that I don't want my daughter around other... lesbianish people."

"I don't believe that just came out of your mouth."

"Well, it did, and like I said, you better not have my damn daughter around them d–"

"Whoa, Xavier, this is not the time. You need to get over it and calm down."

Olivia puts her head down on the table. I try to lift her chin, but she tilts her head away from me. Xavier is still talking shit. Going on and on about how all of this is my fault, and how he could have had a happy family if I'd been truthful.

Softly, but as firmly as possible, I say, "We are not going to do this, Xavier—not now, not ever. That doesn't have anything to do with her well-being."

"I don't want my child introduced to that lifestyle."

"What are you talking about?"

"You're not going to mess her up."

"Lesbians aren't detrimental to children. You sound silly."

"But you heard me."

"You do realize that's like saying you don't want to have her around money."

"What?"

"You can't avoid it... and what you gonna do if she likes girls, huh? Then what?"

"Like I said—"

I cut him off. "What you gonna do about it, if I do have her around women huh? There's nothing you can do, so just stop it."

Xavier stands up. I throw my napkin down and follow suit like we're about to square off. Olivia yells, "Daddy!" snapping my attention to her. I tell Xavier to pay the bill, then I grab Olivia's hand and make my way to the car. Olivia and I are quiet once in the car. I send Xavier a text telling him that I'm taking Olivia to get her nails done and I will have her back to him by 7 pm.

I know that it's my fault my family is in this position, but I thought I was doing the right thing by coming out to Xavier.

When I met him, I was a server in Monroeville, a city about twenty minutes away from Pittsburgh.

Xavier would come into the diner once a week for lunch and I quickly fell for him. Something about him always made me smile — come to think of it, it was his smile.

Growing up in foster care, I hardly ever saw people exhibit genuine happiness. There were a lot of fictitious smiles to get through the days but never smiles of pure joy. Going through foster care and adoption is hard on both sides. The kids don't know what kind of house they're going to walk into, and if they do get a good home, the parents are often wondering if the kid is going to snap on them. Fortunately, I was never adopted — I aged out of the system. When I met Xavier, he was a burst of fresh air for me, therapeutic almost. He became my best friend and showed me what love is. Our story was as fairy tale as it gets until I fucked it up. If I could have predicted what was coming, I would have skipped that fateful Valentine's Day altogether.

February 14, 2007

The snow outside is horrendous! Most of Pennsylvania is under a severe snowstorm, and we're stuck in this cabin in the Poconos. I've been trying to talk to Xavier for weeks, but the words just haven't come out. My heart rate is picking up. I gently shake him awake. He rolls over onto his side and adjusts the pillow under his head. All I can do is look at him.

"Good morning, beautiful," he says.

The words are stuck in my throat, but I have to do it before I chicken out again. In a groggy voice, he asks, "Nadia, what is it, honey?" He can always tell when something is wrong with me.

Softly I say, "Xavier... honey... I think I'm a lesbian?"

He stretches his arms and legs out, then responds, "Okay, babe, whatever you say."

I'm silent.

He abruptly sits up. "Wait! What did you say?"

"I think—"

"I heard what you said, but what do you mean?"

"I've been thinking about it for a while and--"

His hysterical laughing cuts me off. "That was a good one, honey. Come here." He reaches out and tugs on my T-shirt.

I nervously rub my hands across my mouth. "No, Xav, I'm serious. I think I'm attracted to women."

"It sure as hell didn't seem like it last night." He throws the covers off exposing his nakedness and asks softly, "Have you ever been with a woman?"

"No!"

He stands up, kisses my neck, firmly grasps the back of my head, and whispers in my ear, "Then you're not a lesbian, Nadia." I don't respond. He finds his boxers and puts them on.

While walking away, he smacks me on the ass. "Stop joking around and get back in the bed so we can repeat last night."

I wasn't expecting him to think I'm joking. It's taken me so long to be able to say it aloud.

As he enters the bathroom, I cry out, "Xav, I really need you to hear what I'm saying."

He yells back at me, "Oh, I heard what the fuck you said, but it's not believable." The bathroom door slams. *I think I picked the wrong time to tell him this.*

I go downstairs to the kitchen. Usually, the resort staff delivers breakfast, but they can't because of the snowstorm.

Xavier slowly descends the stairs. He tells me to go sit on the couch. Normally, he doesn't talk to me in a forceful way, which means he's pissed. I wipe my hands, turn off the stove, and comply.

He leans against the brick fireplace with his arms folded. "Okay, honey, what are you talking about?" This comes out of his mouth more calmly than I expected.

I jump right into it, no holds barred. "I have these feelings that I just can't shake."

"How long have you felt this way?"

"I don't know," I say at a low volume.

"Don't give me that. Yes, you do."

"Honey, I don't know."

"What? A couple of months? Years?" He slaps the fireplace. "How long have you felt this way, Nadia?"

"Years, I guess."

He scoffs, "So, what? Do you want a divorce? Is that it?"

I honestly don't know the answer to this question because I haven't thought that far ahead.

"No, Xav, I don't."

"Then why are we talking about this? Do you have a girlfriend?" he questions skeptically.

"No!" I say, my voice moving up a pitch.

He slams his fist on the mantle of the fireplace again. "Who is she, Nadia? And don't you fucking lie to me."

"No one! There's no one."

"Then what makes you think you're gay?"

"I just know, okay."

I stand up, and he tells me to sit back down.

"You're telling me that my wife of nine years is a dyke?"

"Don't say that."

"That's what you are, right? A dyke, a carpet muncher!"

I bury my head in the pillow on my lap.

In a whisper, he asks, "Is it me? Am I not being good to you? 'Cause this shit is crazy as hell right now."

"It's not that. It doesn't have anything to do with you." I need to tell him I've felt this way since I was a teenager. It's something I've tried to ignore, but it's always been there.

"Is it sex? Are you bored? Because we can try some new stuff." There's so much pain in his voice.

"No, it's nothing like that; I love being intimate with you."

He screams, "Then explain to me how in the hell you think you're gay."

Xavier is normally a composed man. He barely yells, not even at Olivia when she's acting up. I walk over and hug him, but he doesn't embrace or push me away. He's stoic.

"Nadia, I love you, but you're really throwing me right now."

"I love you, too. Don't think I don't. I'm just confused because I have these feelings, but I want to be with you."

While pushing me away, he says, "Damn right, you're confused! You love me romantically, love to be with me sexually, but you're a lesbian? Get the fuck outta here! This is bogus."

"I know, I know, it's confusing--"

"So, what? Do you want to have a threesome or something? Is that it, because it's not fucking happening."

"No, that's not what I want. I've never even thought about a threesome."

"I can't deal with this shit right now. I'm going back to bed, and when I wake up, you need to have an explanation for me. You need to figure out what you want because I'm not going to play games with you. Either you're in or you're out."

"Xav—" he throws his hand up to silence me as he proceeds up the stairs.

When he's almost to the top, he abruptly turns around. "Who is she?"

"What?"

"What's the name of the woman you're fucking?"

"Xaaaav, there is no one else."
He sits on the couch. I follow suit.

"I'm not cheating on you."

"No, Nadia, I want to know where this is coming from. People don't just make that shit up."

"Xavier—"

"I'm not going to ask you again."

I take a deep breath and press my tongue against the roof of my mouth to stop myself from crying. "What do you want to know?"

"Tell me about the first time you felt this... these feelings."

"Is that necessary?"

"Yes, and we have all day, so talk."

"Uh, I don't know. I guess I first realized that women aroused me in high school."

"What happened?"

"I mean, what do you want to know?"

"Everything."

"Why?"

He screams and jumps to his feet, "Because my fucking wife of nine years is telling me she's a dyke, and I want to know why."

"Don't call me that."

His frustration erupts again and he screams, "Woman..."

I know that I need to stop beating around the bush so I divulge, "I was attracted to a young lady who turned my last year of high school into a living hell, so I suppressed the feelings, okay?"

"And?"

I drop my voice to whisper. "I mean, what is it you want to know? I fell for a girl and got my heart broken?"

He screams back with agitation, "You've told me nothing, Nadia. Stop playing games."

As firmly as I can, I say, "I'm not going to explain all of that, Xavier!"

He sits on the couch and clasps his hands in front of his face. "Oh, yes you are because I need an explanation. You're just gonna come out of your mouth with 'I'm a lesbian,' and I'm supposed to accept it and move on? You got me messed up."

I begin to cry. My last year of high school was hell and he has no idea.

"Don't make me, Xav."

"Talk, Nadia!"

With as little detail as possible, I tell my husband about my first sexual encounter with a female.

"Carly was the first female I was attracted to and the first I ever had a real connection with. I didn't understand my feelings back then, but every time

Carly touched me, I became uncomfortable but not in a bad way. Later, I realized I was lusting after her." I move to stand next to him.

"Tell me about Carly," he says.

"She was my co-runner. Our run times were close, so our coach paired us to enhance each other's abilities. The night before semi-regionals, Carly asked me if I wanted to spend the night at her house instead of at the group home. I was all for it because I wouldn't have to get up as early... Carly and I had spent time together, but never at her house, never alone. The most private time we ever had was on the bus to and from meets. Sometimes, we would fall asleep on each other, but I was too nervous to try something with her." I pause for a long time.

"So, that's it? Because you had a crush, you think you're a lesbian? Kids have weird crushes when they're developing sexually."

"No, it's a little more complicated than that."

"Well, then what are you leaving out?"

"I really don't want to go through all this." I move away from him back to the couch and hang my head.

"Well, you're going to because I don't understand, and we've got all damn day."

I pause and rub my hands across my face, then I blurt out: "She aroused me sexually. When I stayed at her house that night, my feelings were confirmed. That's it. Nothing else happened."

He screams, "Stop fucking around, Nadia! What makes you think you're gay?" I try to find a way to sugar coat everything that happened, but there is no way to soften this. I opened this can of worms.

"Umm... I guess it all started at practice when Carly and I were stretching. Her practice shorts were too big for her that day, and she didn't have her running tights on."

Xavier abruptly moves away from the fireplace to the window.

"When we were stretching, her shorts gaped open, and I could see the impression of her vagina. I had gotten wet before, but what was going on in my panties was more than I could explain. Each time she pushed her legs further apart, my heart rate picked up."

I try not to look at him directly as I tell him of how my attraction to Carly developed.

"Every time Carly would touch my arm or legs when we stretched my wetness increased. I was so aroused that I masturbated in her shower. There was no way I was going to be able to sleep comfortably next to the girl I'd been fantasizing about all day." I pause.

He motions for me to keep talking.

"Why, Xav? This is unnecessary. Just let it go."

"Woman."

"Fine, but remember — you asked." I start speaking fast. "Seeing her vagina peek in and out of her shorts was doing something strange to me. I can't explain it. It was like like something clicked inside of me. I wanted her in every way. The way she smelled was different, everything was different. I wanted to kiss her, stick my fingers inside her. I felt like I never wanted to leave her side again.

"That day was the first time I had what felt like an orgasm while urinating. Back then, I didn't know what was happening. All I knew was that I had an extreme sensation that made me want to scream.

"At her house that night, we talked about the meet the next day before she went to take her shower. While she was bathing, I went downstairs. Her mother told me she forgot to get snacks for the team, so she was going to run to the store. Before going back into Carly's room, I knocked on the bathroom door to let her know her mom had left. She couldn't hear what I was saying, so she told me to come in. I anxiously stood by the door relaying the message. Carly pulled the shower curtain back and told me to hand her the face wash. I turned in her direction with my head down. She asked me what was wrong, had I never seen a naked person before? I remember thinking, *Yeah, but never a beautiful girl with wet hair draping her shoulders, with soap bubbles sporadically covering her, water flowing down her body, or with erect nipples. I've never followed the water line down to a pussy that I want to taste.* I handed her the face wash and ran back to her room. I sprawled out on the floor and screamed into my sweatshirt.

Xavier's eyes are glossy and he keeps pacing back and forth. "Do you want me to stop?"
He shakes his head no. I realize I got caught up and may have disclosed too much.

"I think I've told you enough."

Sounding dejected he mumbles out, "I'll tell you when I've heard enough."

I continue. "Carly got out of the shower and came into the room with just a towel on. She asked me to go get her a Gatorade. When I came back into the room, she was wearing a camisole, and what must have been the smallest pair of boy shorts she owned.

I plopped down on the bed beside her and tried to ignore how sexy she was. She rolled over onto her side and pushed my hair out of my face. The softness of her touch made me tense up. I didn't know what to do, so I told her I was sleepy.

"Underneath the covers felt like a furnace. It didn't take long for Carly to slide her leg over and make contact with mine. My breathing deepened, and she told me to relax. We were both lying on our backs, and I had my hands on my stomach. Her legs slid further apart.

"All she said was 'go with it' before picking my hand up and sliding my fingers between her legs. It was warm and slippery inside her shorts, and I was on fire. After a few moments of rubbing her pussy, Carly got up on her knees, pulled the straps of her camisole down over her shoulders, and then she leaned down and started kissing me. It was the first time I'd felt that way from a kiss. Relent was all I could do."

Xavier turns around and gazes out of the window. "Are you cold? You should put more clothing on if you are going to stand by the window."

"I'm fine, keep talking"

"Carly placed my hands on her breasts and started sucking on my neck. I slid her hand in between my legs, and I almost came. She pulled her hand away, rolled onto her back, and pulled me on top of her. I started sucking on her breast. She lifted her hips and started grinding into my pelvis. All of it felt familiar somehow, almost natural. I asked if I could taste her. She replied, 'Only if you let me eat your pussy first!' We took the rest of our clothes off, and I sat on the edge of the bed, spread eagle. Carly dropped to her knees and softly kissed my clit. I remember feeling like I was melting into the bed. Unfortunately, the sound of a car door closing cut our moment short. Her parents were back and my chance of sleeping with Carly disappeared.

"If I wasn't already in love with Carly, I definitely was then. Well, as much as someone could be in a one-sided relationship. Carly was my best friend, and our sexual tension was through the roof, but as fast as we ascended into our sexual play, the descent into hurt and pain was faster."

"What do you mean?" Xavier asks with inquisition. He doesn't seem to be as mad at me, maybe he truly wants to understand. He is not pacing as much, but he still won't look at me. On occasion, he will change his posture by unfolding his arms and leaning against the window pane.

"Carly and I made it to regionals, and everything was perfect in my small world until the bus ride home from the meet. I fell asleep next to her with my hand on the bottom of her stomach. We were startled awake by the whole team giggling and a boy named Mitchell taking photos of us. Carly went off, saying, 'What the fuck are you doing?! Are you gay? Are you a dyke, Nadia?'

"I went into shock. She berated me in front of everyone. The entire team started chanting *Dyke, dyke, dyke!* before the coach broke up the fiasco.

"Things really went sour the next day at school. I tried to say hello to Carly, but everyone around us burst out laughing. Boys and girls taunted me endlessly. Until graduation two months later, life felt like hell on earth. I was officially the school lesbian, and everyone let it be known constantly. If it weren't for the fact that I was eighteen and would've been kicked out of the group home for not attending school, I probably would have dropped out. It was awful."

Xavier doesn't say anything, I want him to turn and look at me. I want him to acknowledge the pain I endured, but he is closed off. "Xavier, look at me." He takes a deep breath. I watch as his rib cage expands and his shoulders draw up, I want to go over and caress his back, but I'm afraid to touch him. I don't know how he will react, thus far he's been passive aggressive by keeping his back toward me and I don't want him to explode with anger. I've never been afraid of Xavier but I've never seen this coldness from him, so I don't know what to expect.

He says, "Continue."

"Xav, look at me please."

He unfolds his arms and leans on the window pane. "Continue."

"After that, I tried not to think about women in a sexual way. I became angry and started lashing out at everyone. The woman who ran the group home tried to get me to join the military, but right after graduation, I left and moved to Monroeville. Then I met you and fell in love, and I'm still in love with you. You changed my life, and I am grateful for that."

He finally turns around to look at me. I look down and see that he's trying to cover up a semi-erection. He walks over toward the fireplace.

"None of what I've just said changes my feelings for you. I just had to get it off my chest, and I did that."

"So, that's it, huh? You really like girls?"

We're silent, and his erection is steadily fading so I seize the moment. I need him to know I'm still attracted to him.

In an act of submission, I crawl over to him and kiss the top of his foot, then position myself on my knees. I slide his boxers down and after kissing his hip bone he tries to resist but I'm holding his penis. I slide my tongue down to his balls. He tries to push me away, but I grab the head of his dick with my hand and say, "Let me."

Before he can respond, I put his left nut in my mouth because it seems to be the more sensitive of the two. I suck on it and stick my tongue out so I can stroke his scrotum. He finally relaxes. I focus on making him fully hard. I slide my tongue up the bottom of his shaft, and when I reach the tip, I change up my soft and sensual method and deep throat him. But I pull away after a few strokes to catch my breath.

He puts his hand on my head, "Don't stop."

After about five minutes, I place Xavier's hands on my ears, a signal to let him know he's in charge. I deep throat him again. He widens his stance and begins thrusting hard. I have to hold onto the fireplace to brace myself, and he uses my ears as an anchor. "Tell me you love me. Tell me you love sucking my dick," he grunts out.

I tap his thigh to signal he's been choking me too long, but he doesn't stop pushing toward the back of my throat.

As he climaxes, there's no courtesy of pulling out and shooting wherever it lands. He deliberately cums in my mouth and, as a reflex, I swallow. I continue sucking him until he softens. When I lean back on my heels, I look up at him with puppy dog eyes; he looks down at me with confusion and then leaves me.

After an hour of him being alone and me over-thinking the situation, I go upstairs. I slide beneath the sheets with him and quietly say, "Olivia's dance instructor," before kissing between his shoulder blades.

"What?"

"That's who I have a crush on now. We haven't done anything, though. I promise." The way his body tenses makes me realize I shouldn't have said it, but I need to put all my cards on the table.

"The lady Olivia has been having private lessons with?"

"Xav, nothing has happened with her, I swear."

"The woman that Olivia just had to train with? That's $100 a session."

I nod my head.

"Enough. I can't take it anymore. Go pack your shit. I can't stand to be here with you any longer. And you tell me this on Valentine's Day, of all days?"

"But we're stuck--" he rolls his eyes and slams his fist into the pillow. He tells me we're done and then climbs out of bed, tears forming in his eyes.

"Xav, can we talk about it?"

In the saddest voice I've ever heard, he says, "There's nothing to talk about. You'll never be happy with me because you're a lesbian." He steps onto the patio into the cold. I hand him a robe and make my way downstairs with a blanket.

My life turned upside when we returned to Monroeville.

* * *

Since Olivia and I stormed out of the restaurant, there's been nothing but silence.

Olivia asks, "Are you a lesbian?" Her direct question surprises me.

"Olivia, first let me apologize for our behavior. Your father and I were very foolish."

"Yeah, you two do something to each other."

"I know, honey, and I'm sorry. That argument had nothing to do with you. And yes, I am a lesbian."

"Is that why Dad is so mad?

"Yes."

"Can you make him happy by not being a lesbian?"

"It's not that simple, love. You can't change your sexual orientation, just like you can't change your skin color."

"But you can change your skin color."

I'm stumped. I didn't see that coming. "You're right, honey. I guess you can change anything about yourself nowadays.

"Dad said you have to be careful when you choose who you love."

"That's true."

"Oh, I think I get it. You like to have sex with girls."

I pull the car over and park in a gas station's lot. I turn around to look at her. She is twirling her hair around her finger. "Wait! Who told you about sex?"

"Grandma."

"What did she say to you?"

"That as I get older, I will start to have these feelings."

"What kind of feelings?" I stare at her in the rearview mirror.

"She said that in my belly, I will want to do things. But I'll be confused in my head, so I have to follow my heart above anything else."

"That's what she said sex is?"

"No, she said sex is when you touch another's private parts and they touch yours."

I clear my throat. "Do you have any questions?"

"Not really." She stares out of the window and starts rubbing her hands together. When she was younger she used to do that when she was nervous.

"Honey, what's wrong?"

"Mommy, can I go back to Baltimore with you?"

Asking why doesn't matter; all I needed was to hear those words.

I have a sleepless night planning my approach when I file custody papers in the morning. Xavier will have a harder time fighting me on custody this time. When we were divorcing, I didn't have the means to take care of her. But now, since I've been working for Mrs. Spady, I've saved up a decent chunk of change.

The judge gave everything to Xavier and told me I had thirty days to evacuate my home. It's amazing how the justice system is still so bigoted. I have always been a good mother and wife, but because I like women and was broke, the courts found me to be unfit.

I went into shock for a couple days, and that turned into a severe depression. I tried to find work, but after not working for seven years and having no current address, I couldn't find a job. I couldn't even get into a women's shelter because I didn't have a child with me. How every shelter managed to be full still baffles me.

After three months of hoping Xavier would come to his senses, I accepted my situation. Maybe I should've thought about the consequences before coming out, but I've always been too honest. People don't really want to hear the truth; they only like to hear the things that pacify them.

9

NADIA cont'd

I bury my face in my jacket, lean against the plane window, and sob. Eleven days into my trip, I have to return home. Rosa frantically called me this morning saying Mrs. Spady had a heart attack and hit her head.

The man in the seat beside me asks if I'm all right and offers me a pill to calm my nerves. I decline by shaking my head no.

I collect myself enough to say, "I'll be all right," even though I'm falling apart on the inside. The thought of losing Mrs. Spady, the only mother figure I've had in my life, is crushing me. If it weren't for her, I don't know where I'd be. She literally pulled me from the streets and molded me into a strong woman.

The balding man attempts to extend our conversation; I oblige him.

"Are you afraid of flying?" he asks.

"No," I murmur. "My boss is dying."

"Sorry to hear that."

I don't respond.

"Your boss must be a great person to have you this emotional."

I inhale deeply and focus on steadying my quivering lips. "She really is. Mrs. Spady is more like a mother to me than a boss."

"Well, hopefully, she'll pull through," he says while unfolding a tissue.

"I don't know what I'm gonna do if she passes." The floodgate to my tears opens.

"You have to continue to live."

"I'm alive because of her, though. If she had— If she hadn't..." I let out a high-pitched squeal drawing the attention of the flight attendant my way. I try to compose myself.

"Try not to get too worked up."

"I don't think I can talk about this."

"And you don't have to, but if you want to I have a great listening ear. I'm life coach Brad Eckert by the way."

"Life coach?" Seeing the skepticism on my face, he pulls out his business card. I examine it. "Well, Brad, I may actually have to hire you one day."

"Being that we're stuck on this flight together..." He looks at his watch. "I guess I can give you a free thirty-minute session." I force myself to smile.

Brad asks how Mrs. Spady saved my life, and something about the way he asks makes it feel okay to open up.

"I get sad when I think about that time in my life," I tell him. "It was a really dark period for me."

He leans his shoulders forward and tries to look me in the eye. "That's because you're focusing on the bad things that got you into that situation, rather than how far you've come since that moment."

I think about that, then acknowledge that he's right.

"Tell me about your first meeting with her. What's your name, by the way?"

"Nadia."

"Well, Nadia, when did you meet Mrs. Spady?"

"After my divorce, while I was homeless."

He adjusts his glasses and clears his throat.

"You were homeless?"

"Yes."

"Wow." After the awkward silence, I start talking about what happened.

"It's amazing how fast things change in life. Before living on the streets, I never thought twice about walking into a restaurant because of the way I was dressed, or because my scent might be offensive. It wasn't like I didn't want to be clean—most places banned me for stealing too many napkins and rolls of tissue, which I only wanted to make myself look a little more presentable."

"Sorry, you went through that."

"It was horrible, but then I met Mrs. Spady, and she changed my life."

"How so?"

"On the day we met, I was giving myself a pep talk outside of a diner. I was telling myself, *Pull it together. Go in there, ask for an application, and leave as fast as possible. Don't linger.*"

"Interesting."

"I'd been standing there for about thirty minutes, waiting for the crowd in the diner to shrink so I wouldn't embarrass myself. Anyway, a family of three was exiting the restaurant, so I opened the door for them. The little boy stopped and asked if I wanted to go home with them. His mother quickly yanked him to her side and said, 'Leave that woman alone.' The father gave me a five-dollar bill. I felt like that was a blessing, so I pepped up a bit. I tucked in my gray long-john shirt, which was about three sizes too big, put my stringy strands of hair into a rubber band, and walked into the diner."

I pause so Brad and I can order drinks. Right after the flight attendant turns toward the seat opposite us, Brad urgently says, "Keep going, Nadia. I feel like you need to let this out."

"That was way too descriptive. I feel like I'm talking too much."

"It's fine. Tell me as much detail as possible."

"Are you sure?"

"Yes! So, what happened next?"

"Someone was placing a to-go order, and I was behind him, rocking back and forth, hoping to get an application. I asked for numerous applications, but it got harder every day because my appearance was deteriorating. I assume most people thought I was a drug addict. I wasn't able to keep myself clean the way I wanted to.

"When I got to the counter, the young lady covered her nose with two of her fingers. I wanted to run away, but I swallowed my pride and said, 'Excuse me. Do you all… Are you all hiring?' The girl hurriedly explained that they weren't. I started begging for a chance."

"I looked to my right, and an older woman was glaring at me."

"Was the lady Mrs. Spady?"

I nod my head yes. "She started fussing at me. 'Don't badger that young woman. She answered your question, now move on.' I said to Mrs. Spady, 'But I know they're hiring.' Mrs. Spady said, 'She clearly told you they're not.' I tried to explain that I called them earlier that day and asked about open positions, but Mrs. Spady cut me off and asked my name. When I told her, she gasped. She paused, looked at me very hard, and grabbed the side of the countertop. She cleared her throat and then asked, 'Nadia, if I give you a hundred dollars to leave here, what would you do with it?'

"'What?'

"'You heard me. What are you gonna do? Leave here and go shoot up?'

"'Look, I don't want any problems. I'll leave.'

"She said, 'I asked you a question. Now give me an honest answer. Will you go buy drugs? Buy your baby some Top Ramen and smoke the rest?'

"'Don't be condescending to me, lady. That's rude as hell,' I told her."

"What was your answer?" Brad asks.

"I told her I'd go take a bath and buy some clothes, come back here, and ask for a job again. Mrs. Spady handed me a one hundred dollar bill and started crying. She explained that her best friend had just died, and she didn't want me to kill myself with drugs. Then, out of nowhere, a big man—big enough to pick up me and Mrs. Spady at the same time—walked up and escorted her away. I left the diner feeling dejected about the job, but elated that I would be able to clean myself up."

"What did you buy?" Brad asks. "I've always been curious about homeless people's plight."

"I can't speak for everyone else, but I went to the 100 Pennies clothing store."

"100 Pennies? I've never heard of it."

"I'm not sure it still exists. They sell what the clothing industry would consider severely defective. The stuff that gets rejected from the retail stores that sell the cheapest name brands."

"Oh."

"It all works the same, though—it covers the body."

"You're right about that."

"I went into the store and came out with two new outfits, including shoes, two weeks' worth of underwear, and a buggy to pull around—all for thirteen dollars. Then I made the sixty-minute walk to the truck stop on the outskirts of town."

"That's a long walk. Why so far?"

"It was too far away for me to frequent and end up getting banned because I was bathing in the bathroom or using too many paper towels."

"I understand."

"That ten-minute shower felt like heaven on earth."

"I bet."

"I wanted to take two, but I couldn't waste the money. It felt like a new day. I remember standing in front of the store and looking to the left and right. To the right was Philly. I could go back there and stay on the beaten path, or I could go to the left and see what was out there. After contemplating the issue for a few moments, something told me to go back toward downtown, and I'm glad I did."

"Because you met Mrs. Spady?"

"Exactly. As I started walking back to Philly, a car drove past me and made a U-turn. I almost took off running, but kept my cool."

"Wow, Nadia. You never know what someone has been through."

"And I have been through a lot."

"And you have overcome it. That's the beauty of your life."

I shrug my shoulders.

Brad continues to be inquisitive. "So, what happened?"

"I was casually walking, and I heard, 'Young lady, come here.' I recognized the voice to be that of the woman from the diner. I said a prayer and walked toward the car, and I'll be damned if God didn't answer my prayer right then because my life changed forever. When we arrived back in the city, Mrs. Spady got me a hotel room. I didn't know what to do with myself, so I walked to the middle of the room, collapsed on the floor, and fell asleep.

"She even ordered me food. I hadn't seen that much food in a while. I became so overwhelmed that I had to take a shower to calm myself. While looking in the mirror, I noticed how frail I'd become.

"The next morning, I was dressed by 7:00 a.m. Jonathan, Mrs. Spady's driver, came by at 6:15 a.m. and told me I was going to accompany Mrs. Spady to a business meeting as her assistant. He handed me some clothes and a portfolio and then told me to read up because the presentation was at 10 a.m."

"Just like that, your life changed overnight."

"Yep. I ended up accompanying Mrs. Spady to what turned out to be a job interview."

"Wait. She pulled you off the streets and gave you a job the next day?"

"I told you she saved my life."

"So, what was your presentation about?"

"A horse farm. She wanted to build one, but I convinced her to build a boarding lodge instead of buying a bunch of horses."

"A bunch of horses? Is this lady rich?"

"Yes, but I don't know how much she's worth."

"Now I understand why you're so emotional about her."

"Outside of my ex-husband and daughter, she's the only person I've had an emotional bond with."

"Well, hopefully, she will be okay."

"I hope so."

The pilot announces our landing, and I gaze out of the window for the last few minutes of the flight. Just before we part ways, Brad puts his hand on my shoulder. "Remember to live, Nadia. And you have my card if you ever want to find me."

Mrs. Spady has been the single most important person in my life. She has built me into a woman, gave me stability, and a job. She is my world. I don't know how I will live without her.

10

Jonathan picks me up from the airport and rushes me to the hospital. I break down when I see Mrs. Spady lying in the bed with her eyes closed, tubes up her nostrils, and her head wrapped in white gauze. Because of her age and the head injury, the doctors are keeping her in a coma. Jonathan leaves to check on the house affairs and I settle in for the night underneath the hospital room window.

Dear Purple Book:

I keep asking God to please let her be all right. Ms. Spady is the only parental figure I've known, and I don't know what I'll do without her. Numerous times, I asked her to walk on the path in the backyard instead of that damn treadmill, but she refused. Stubbornness has gotten the best of her. But I need her to be okay. I keep losing everything. I try to be a good person, but everything continuously falls apart. I was born to an alcoholic father with priors, and a mother with other priorities, and so Mrs. Spady is the only true mother figure I've known.

Sometimes I wonder about my parents. The only thing I know about them came from a letter a social worker gave me when I was twelve. I remember my mother wrote that she and my father were together for seven years, but he drank too much and things were just getting started in her life when she got pregnant, so she put me up for adoption. In a fit, I tore up the letter and put it in the trash before making it to the end. If I could take back any moment in my life, it would be that one. It was the only piece of her I had, and ironically, I threw it away just like she threw me away.

As I got older, I reconciled my circumstances by telling myself that I am here for a reason. My parents were together for seven years, and I am the one drunken sperm that was sober enough to find an egg. After reading and destroying that letter, I became an angry child, which is probably why I switched foster homes so much. It wasn't until I was about fifteen that I let some of the anger go, but I always kept my guard up. Even if I was the perfect child, my fate was always at someone else's discretion. Like the last family that fostered me. In the blink of an eye, they got rid of me.

I was with the Drast family for two years, until my foster brother and I fooled around and his parents found out. They thought I was the cause of his sexual activity, and they sent me back to the group home. We only messed around once, as an experimental thing, but it was enough to get me fired from another family. His parents wanted to prevent anything further from happening, which is understandable, but it still hurt. It worked out for the best, though, because I was too attached to them. They were the first group of people who made me feel like part of the family.

But then, Mrs. Spady found me and started referring to me as her daughter. She never refers to any of her other employees this way, but I don't mind because it makes me smile. She says I remind her of a great part of her life. I still haven't figured out what that means, but I don't pry because she is so private. If she doesn't pull through, who's going to... ... I have to stop now, getting too emotional.

*

"What's going on, where am I?"

Mrs. Spady's voice startles me. My journal slides from my lap to the floor. I jump up and run to the bed. I hit the call button for the nurse and encourage Mrs. Spady to stop talking. I look at my phone: Wednesday, July 6, 2011, 8:27 a.m. I don't know when I fell asleep. The last time I looked at the clock, it was three hours ago, when they decreased the sedative medication so she could wake up naturally.

The nurse comes into the room and checks Mrs. Spady's vitals and cognitive ability. She tells Mrs. Spady about her brain injury and how, at her age, she could rapidly decline, which is why they've kept her sedated. The nurse tells me that Mrs. Spady needs to go through a series of tests, and they suggest I go home to freshen up.

*

I'm about to step into the shower when I receive a frantic call to return to the hospital. I rush back and the nurse intercepts me as I'm about to enter the room.

"What happened?"

The nurse says, "We are not sure, but shortly after you left, she began to crash. But we've stabilized her."

I drop to my knees and begin to pray.

The sun is going down when I hear, "Nadia." I jump to my feet.

"Mrs. Spady, don't talk, don't talk."

Through labored breathing, she says, "I've... been... in mourning, hoping that my days wouldn't last much longer... my heart was broken. I loved them both." I crouch next to the hospital bed. I try to shush her, but she gives me the listen-to-me look.

Mrs. Spady whispers, "Nadia, it's time, but I have to... I'm tired... I have to tell you—" She pauses to catch her breath. When she starts speaking again, her voice is groggy. The heart monitor slows. I begin to cry hysterically.

Through gasps of air, she continues, "Nadia, don't be mad... Go get your girl if you feel she likes the one... They aren't going to make it."

"What are you talking about?"

"Laila... and the other woman... they aren't going to make it."

I tell her to stop talking and to focus on her breathing. She squeezes my hand and struggles to get it free again. Her hand begins to shake uncontrollably, "Nadia, don't be mad. Forgive in your—" She taps on her heart, then a tear falls from her eye. "I adopted you for Naida..."

"Naida Marie always loved you." Then she fades away.

"Naida... Who's Naida? Mrs. Spady, don't go. I need you." Her eyes are closing. I try to pull them open and say her name repeatedly. Jonathan tries to pull me away.

"No!" I scream while shaking her. The nurse comes in and grabs my arms. I slide to the floor and fall apart. Jonathan picks me up and carries me to the waiting room. The nurse closes the blinds and I feel the energy around me drain away. She is gone.

* * *

One month later

Jonathan has been my saving grace since Mrs. Spady passed away. A month ago today, he sent in a team of lawyers—the best in the country—Mrs. Spady's suit tailor, and a mobile spa to get me ready for the custody hearing.

I had to bring out an army to face Xavier's police force, and I'm glad I did because I wasn't ready for what happened on that day—I won custody! Two days later, Olivia and I were on a plane to Georgia, because that's where she wanted to go for a vacation. We fed a giraffe at the zoo, visited the MLK memorial, went to Six Flags, and then headed back to Baltimore. I can take Olivia to do anything that she wants because Mrs. Spady left me everything, outside of the allotment for her other staff.

I've been lonely without her, but Olivia has been keeping me busy. In trying to learn her all over again, I've been spoiling her like crazy. I know I shouldn't, but I can't help it. Sometimes I give in to her out of guilt, but mostly I want to give her the world. I didn't think I'd ever get to raise her full-time again.

Rosa announces over the intercom that Olivia's history teacher is here. I look at the clock. The contractors will be at my condo in two hours. I go downstairs into the office, kiss Olivia on her head, tell her to pay attention today, and if she gets a good report we can bake cookies when I come home later.

11

NADIA
Sept 12, 2011

As the guy is standing here explaining that his co-worker went to the WAWA because his stomach is upset, I'm wondering why in the hell I bought all this shit I don't need. I should have canceled the order, but honestly, with everything going on, I forgot I ordered it. Damn infomercials!

They're installing a specialized fish tank with built in surveillance cameras that I ordered five months ago but will hardly need anymore because I live in Mrs. Spady's mansion full-time now.

I haven't seen Laila in months, but revamping my surroundings, shopping, running, and repeating isn't easing my pain. Nevertheless, I can't bring myself to answer her calls or fulfill her requests to meet because I know she will hurt me again.

By the time the technician has completed the installation in the living room his co-worker still hasn't arrived. I'm half paying attention to his explanation on how to activate and change the memory cards when the doorbell rings. I open it and immediately close it. I'm in shock. There's no way, it's been like ten years. It can't be. I whisper, "You've got to be fucking kidding me," then I slowly open the door again.

"Hello, Nadia."

All I can say is "Umm?" while shaking my head in disbelief.

"I'm glad I found you. I wasn't sure if..." She stops and switches to an apology. "Please forgive me for just showing up like this, but do you have a minute?"

I'm stunned.

The elevator dings before I can answer her. The other technician is here. God must be feeling some type of way about me right now. First, the Laila fallout, then Mrs. Spady died, now this chick shows up literally out of nowhere. I get my shit together, pull the technician inside, tell her to leave and then slam the door shut.

Forty-five minutes later, when the work is completed, I walk the technicians into the hallway. Carly is seated next to the elevator across from my apartment.

"I thought you left," I say.

She stands and straightens her clothes. "I couldn't bring myself to walk away." Her voice is raspier than I remember.

"What are you doing here?" I say sharply.

"I've been looking for you for like two years."

"Why?"

"You cross my mind all the time. After I saw you on TV, I decided to find you."

"And now that you have?"

"I want to tell you I'm sorry."

I squint and say, "You went on a two-year search to say sorry?"

Carly puts her hands in her pockets and rocks back and forth. That look of innocence that drew me to her when we were teenagers surfaces. I try to ignore her eyes, but I can't stop staring at them. I used to love looking into her green eyes. She says, "I guess so. I mean, I know it's strange, but what happened between us has haunted me for the past sixteen years."

"Yeah, it was fucked up. You know you came onto me, Carly, and then you acted like you had no idea about my sexuality. I thought if I ever saw you again I would slap the shit out of you, but there's no point because it's not gonna change how you made me feel."

"Nadia, I'm sorry. I didn't know what to do, I was trying to hide it, and I don't know... I was young and dumb."

One of my neighbors comes into the hall, which stops me from saying something nasty to Carly.

"Look, I have to go pick some food up for my daughter. Is there anything else?"

"Nadia, I'm sorry—"

"I got it!"

"Can we meet up sometime and talk?" I think about it for a moment and decide I need to figure out what she wants and get her out of my life as soon as possible.

I invite her to Panera Bread with me so I can control our interactions. She has me very flustered right now and my emotions are all over the place. I want to catch up with her, but she also brought up a lot of dormant feelings. I'd never felt that kind of hurt before.

"I can't believe you're sitting in my car right now."

"I know, right? After all these years, we've been living thirty miles apart."

"I'm a little in shock right now, Carly. I never expected to cross paths with you again."

"I guess the stars aligned."

I scoff at her. "The stars aligned?"

"What?"

"We didn't just randomly cross paths. You sought me out."

"I just wanted to catch up with you."

"So what happened when you saw me on TV?"

"I couldn't believe my eyes, and it dawned on me that your last name was probably different."

"What was I doing?"

"When?"

"When you saw me on TV — what was I doing?"

"The first time, you were looking up at the building. The second time you were holding a woman's hand. Is she your girlfriend?"

I tighten my grip on the steering wheel. "No, she's not."

"Oh." Carly pauses. "That situation looked... umm..."

"It's a hot fucking mess is what it is."

Carly starts laughing. "I bet."

Awkward silence finds us, and I shake my head at this situation. I've been trying hard to bite my tongue; everything in me wants to curse her out. Carly looks at me and adjusts her position by pressing her left shoulder into the seat so she can face me more directly. "You still make that noise when you're agitated."

"What noise?"

"That deep breathing, along with the sucking of your teeth."

"You fucked up my last months of high school, Carly Jackson, and yes it still bothers me, but I forgive you." Before she can respond, I ask her about her relationship status.

"Umm, I'm in a relationship with a woman," she says.

I look at her and sarcastically say, "Oh, so you turned out to be gay!"

"I guess so."

"How ironic!"

She taps my hand excitedly. I look at her skeptically. "OMG, Nadia. Tell me what you've been up too. Every day, I've wondered if you were okay. It looks like things turned out amazing for you."

"I wish I could say everything is perfect, but my life is fucking complicated, Carly."

"Tell me about it," she mutters. "Sometimes I wish I was a kid again."

I sense pain in her voice but I'm not going to pry. "So, Carly Jackson! I like your androgynous look."

She smiles and rubs her hands across her legs. "It's been a long time, Nadia, but I still feel connected to you."

"And this may be a little fucked up, but I feel indifferent. I mean, I'm trying to digest this right now. I blocked you from my mind, and today you show up out of the blue."

"Sorry for popping up, but you never know what tomorrow will bring, and I needed to apologize to you."

"Well, thank you for that, but I don't know about letting you back into my life."

"And that's understandable. I was young and what I did was fucked up."

"Come on, we have to get out the car and go in."

Carly grabs my hand as I open the restaurant door. Her eyes are teary. "Nadia, if I never see you again, know that I am truly sorry and I didn't understand the impact my actions would have."

I'm silent for a moment too long because she asks if I am all right.

I delay responding and ask, "Do you want some food?"

"Sure."

I marinate on what she said while waiting in line. When we get back in the car, I say, "Carly, you cannot still love me. You are in love with who I used to be, and what could have been, but trust me, we are both very different now. So, if you have any love, it's based on an idea."

"You're probably right, but either way, my heart is still fond of you. That didn't change."
She breaks the awkward moment by asking, "Do you have to pick your daughter up?"

"No, Jonathan is going to get her."

"Is that your husband?"

"I'm divorced. Jonathan is our driver."

She laughs. "Driver?"

"What's funny?"

"Well, a couple of things. One, it must be a lot of money that you inherited because your daughter has a driver. Two, you drive a Bentley and that condo looks expensive. I'm surprised you don't have a doorman. And three, it's funny how life works out. Your ex-husband is probably pissed that you're rich, and me... I'm a manager at Burger King.

"Well, that's not a bad gig."

"It's not cookie-cutter either."

"Whoa. You think I have a glamorous life? Most of my life has been tragic, and I am just now catching a break."

"Calm down. I didn't mean anything by it. You look paid, that's all."

"Trust—I'm surprised every morning when I wake up. This lady left me some money when she passed away, and I don't know, not much has changed outside of my bank account balance."

"Well, at least now you have the means to change your life."

"What do you mean?"

"A lot of people want more out of life and can't catch a break."

"But money can't make you happy, cause I'm n-" I stop myself from divulging my problems to her.

"Nadia, you know that doesn't happen, right? People randomly leaving someone money? So, in that sense, you are privileged."

"I guess you're right."

When we arrive back at my condominium, I ask Carly what side of the building she parked on.

As I drive around the corner, I see Laila leaning on her car. "Shit," I say.

"What?"

"Hold on for a second." I call Olivia and tell her I got a call from the horse ranch, and that I will be home late, and to have Jonathan take her to get whatever she wants to eat.

I hear Carly whisper, "Horse ranch? Wow!"

I start talking fast once I'm off the phone. "Look, I know what I'm about to ask is fucked up, but that's the woman you saw me on TV with."

"You need me to stay?"

"I need to use you. When we get out of the car, hug me like we're fucking each other and kiss me on the cheek. On the cheek, okay?! Remember that you have a girlfriend. Then say, 'See you soon.'"

"All of that! Why?"

"Can you please do it?"

"Can I see you again?"

"Can you do it?"

"Can I see you again?"

"Yes, Carly... Will you do it?"

"Can I see you in two days?"

"Ugh. Yes"

"Okay."

When we get out of the car and Laila sees Carly kiss me extra close to my lips, her eyes look like they're going to pop out of her head.

Once Carly is gone, Laila, who usually sashays when she walks, looks like she's about to take off running. I stand in place with my arms crossed.

Laila takes a deep breath and says my name like I'm a child she's about to chastise. "Is she the reason you've been ignoring me?"

I giggle. Only to piss her off, though. "No."

"Who is she?"

"Are you really questioning me?"

"I am."

"Calm down, woman."

"I'm trying to figure out what is going on."

"Why is it your place to figure that out, Laila?" She grunts and balls up her fist.

"I'm going inside. You coming in, or...?"

"Damn right, I am."

"Look, Laila, we are not in a position to be arguing with each other, so if that's what you plan on doing, stay your ass down here."

"I didn't come to argue with you, but I also didn't expect to walk into this."

I roll my eyes and tell her to come on.

On the elevator, she asks me if I'm dating people. I stay as vague as possible. "Would you feel some kind of way if I am? Does the thought of me fucking someone else bother you?"

She closes her eyes tight and flares her nostrils. "Nadia, you sure have changed this past couple of months, you're not as... as—"

"As what? Docile?!"

"Peaceful."

"What? Is it wrong that I've changed since you fucking humiliated me on TV? Changed since getting my daughter back?" My voice cracks. "Changed since Mrs. Spady died? You didn't even come to the funeral, and it's been what? Two and a half months since I last saw you?"

"I'm sorry, okay? And you're right. I don't have any room to judge anything you do."

"You're damn right, you don't." The elevator door opens and Laila follows me inside and sits on the couch. I go to the bathroom to pull myself together. I look in the mirror and give myself a pep talk. Say all of the things that have been on your chest. Tell her how you feel and move on with your life. You don't need the drama.

I come out of the bathroom and say, "Okay, Laila, you came over here, so let's talk. No arguing or being sarcastic. Let's really talk."

"Umm... I don't know where to start. Usually, you're so easy to talk to, but it's hard to find the words right now."

"I'm still easy to talk to. It's your guilt that has you tongue-tied. And you know what? You should feel guilty."

"I don't want you to be pissed forever."

"I have the right to be pissed as long as I want to. You're lucky I'm not going berserk on you like I'd planned." Laila raises her eyebrows. "That's right, I've been thinking of something fucked up I could do to get back at you."

"Damn, really?"

"Yes, but karma is a bitch, so I really don't have to do anything,"

Laila asks me if I think we can be friends. Expecting her to blow a gasket, I say, "No, fuck that. I don't want to be your friend. I want to fuck you."

She responds sarcastically. "Are you sure? Because we're already in a messy situation!"

I wasn't expecting her to match my sarcasm. I have to regroup my thoughts.

"What? You don't think I'll be able to handle it?"

"No, I'm just saying, I don't want you to be a side chick."

I laugh at her, "Dammit, Laila. You already made me a side chick."

She frowns but refrains from responding.

"Go ahead and say it, Laila. Say something slick."

"It wasn't like that, Nadia. I wasn't trying to make you a side chick."

I say, "Hold on, wait a minute. You decided to fuck three people, and you're trying to tell me I wasn't a side chick? Get the fuck outta here."

Laila screams, "I didn't intend on it being that way. Shit just happened."

I throw my hands up. "Shit just happened?! Don't bullshit me, Laila." I stand up and move toward the front door. My emotions are getting the best of me and I blurt out. "You know what? I don't want to keep talking about it. Either we're gonna be fuck buddies or we're not."

Laila asks me if that's all I want. In all honesty, it's not, I wish I could take it back, but I know I can't be connected to her the way I want, so until I can move on, why not have a fuck buddy? The look in her eyes is one of endearment like she truly wants more from me, but I'm not going to let her have it. She's controlled the dynamics of our relationship thus far, now I'm in control.

I say what I know she doesn't want to hear, "Yes, that's all I want."

I've been watching Laila sit silently for about five minutes now. She drew into herself when I told her that lie. Because I lied, and because I'm too prideful to walk it back, I sit silently with her. She starts squeezing her hands together, then suddenly raises her head like she's had an epiphany. She stands and attempts to leave. "All righty then. It is what it is." I beg her to stay while pulling her away from the door. I'm so foolish for letting myself stay involved with her, but my emotions are all tied up. I don't want to let her go.

I place kisses on her neck and justify my actions by telling myself that maybe, just maybe, what Mrs. Spady predicted is true and Laila and Victoria didn't make it. Maybe Laila realized how much she loves me, and that's why she is here.

I quickly strip out of my clothing. She steps back and glares at me. I guide her to the couch. I offer her a chance to leave when I walk into the kitchen to grab a glass of water. She stays.

I walk over to the couch and stand behind her. I look into her eyes and press my finger against her forehead, drawing her head back. Her windpipe moves. I drip the cold water across her neck from right to left, and then splash a dollop onto her breastbone, in what I imagine to be a Fifty Shades of Grey kind-of-way, even though I've never read it. Through a winced flinch, she grabs the glass and says, "I love you."

I respond, "I hate you."

I walk around to the front of the couch, straddle her waist and then forcefully grind my clit on her pelvic bone. I try to be aroused, I try to rouse her by softly kissing her neck, but our chemistry is off. I bite her cheek hard enough for her to wince. She responds by squeezing my ass cheeks. We place our foreheads together and stare into each other's eyes. I fight to hold back my tears. She lets hers run free. I can't stand to see her cry, so I tell her to stay on the couch while I go take a shower.

In the shower, everything wrong about this situation surfaces and I try to cry the feelings away. I'm tired of fighting with her and with myself. When I pull it together and finally exit the shower, Laila comes into the bathroom and asks if I still have any of her things because she wants to take a shower too. Foolish me. I never fully purged her from my life.

She has my emotions are all over the place right now. I want her, but I don't need her in my life. I love her, but I hate what she's done.

While she's in the shower, I lie on the bed and think about whether I really want to rehash things or just let them be. I'm in a good space now and finding myself again. I was an emotional wreck after Mrs. Spady died, and I don't need this drama in my life. I'll just let things progress naturally.

I'm laying on my stomach gazing peacefully out the window when Laila interrupts me by sliding her hand up my leg into my gaped shorts. She grips the middle of my shorts and tugs at them. I close my legs and trap her hand. She tries to wriggle it out. I laugh at her and say, "I've got you in my clutches now." She smacks my outer thigh with her other hand making me scream. Before the sting of the first slap dissipates, she does it again and tells me to turn over. I let go of her hand, turn over onto my side, and fiddle with the sheet. She lifts my hand and strokes it against her pussy hairs, which are still wet from the shower. "Does it feel good?" she asks.

"Yeah. Are you gonna let me taste it?" *Here I go — her pussy does something to me.*

She pushes my hand away playfully. "No!"

Laila walks over to the bed, drops her towel, and fully exposes her pussy by putting one foot on the bed.

I jump to my feet and playfully push her onto the bed. "Yes, you are." I get lost in the moment and we indulge each other for a while, and then she convinces me to go to DC with her. I don't know what I want and I think she knows that, but I mean, she wouldn't be here if she didn't want me right?

*

Watching Laila pull her sushi apart rather than eating it whole feels like old times, I've always found it interesting that she doesn't eat Sushi whole. It's not easy to ignore the fact that she humiliated me on TV, and lied a gazillion times about who she was fucking, but this moment feels nice. She feeds me her last salmon roll and we make our way to Recess karaoke bar. I jokingly ask Laila to sing me a song and she agrees. Usually, when we go to karaoke we end up going back and forth until I give in, then she laughs 'til her stomach hurts because I can't sing worth a dime.

She goes up to the mic, and the DJ randomly picks "I'm Going Down" by Mary J. Blige. She sounds terrible. Reality hits me again. All of this is terrible. When she ends the second verse, I get up and walk out. She runs after me. I make it out of the door and down the street by the time she catches me.

"Laila, what the fuck are we doing? What is this? Everything is just fine and dandy now?," rushes out of my mouth like a freight train.

"See, that's why I love you. You say what you're thinking no matter what."

"Laila, don't patronize me."

"Okay, okay. I know we've been skirting the issue, it's just..." she strokes my elbow. "I wanted us to hang out like old times. I haven't seen you in months, and I couldn't help myself." She grabs my arm. "But it was good, right?"

I walk away. She begs me. "Dia, come here, babe."

"Don't call me Dia!" I tell her to take me home.

In the car, my conscience really starts to eat at me because I know this isn't right. I ask, "Where is Tori?"

"Flying to Miami."

"Oh, so you had a free moment to come interrupt my world."

"It wasn't like that."

"Laila, I'm not gonna play games with you. I'm not a side chick, and I'm not gonna let you make me one." I scream, "Ugh! I'm mad at myself for having sex with you. I'm so fucking gullible. It's not gonna happen again. Trust and believe that."

"I wasn't trying to play games. I thought Tori was cheating on me, so I decided to move on."

"And I was what? A pawn to get her back?"

"No, hell no. I fell for you."

I laugh at her. "Really now? So, when did you get engaged?"

Her hands tighten around the steering wheel, and she puts her head down.

I second-guess my questions. "Wait, answer this. Are you still engaged?"

"Nadia, I'm sorry for everything that has happened."

I say, "Fuck you, Laila," and jump out of the car as soon as we stop at a light. I don't know if I'm more upset with her for acting like everything is all good, or more upset with myself for opening up to her again.

I go into a restaurant and call Jonathan so he can send me a driver. I need to be home with my daughter, anyway. When I get home, Laila is sitting outside the entry gate to my house. Jonathan meets me at the gate and tells me I need closure with Laila. I tell him to have her follow us in, but she only has thirty minutes.

I'm forced to introduce Laila to Livey when we walk in, something I'm not prepared to do. I can tell Livey catches Laila off guard because of the stunned looked on Laila's face, but that's the least of my worries. I need to cut Laila out of my life.

I tell Livey I will visit her room in thirty minutes after my guest leaves. Laila tries to ask me about Livey, but I tell her she doesn't have time for fluff conversation. "It's 8:55. You have until 9:25, so get to talking."

"Can I get something to drink?" she asks.

I roll my eyes at her and ask Rosa to get both of us some water.

"Okay, I guess I'll jump right in."

I respond sarcastically. "That'd be best."

"When we met, Tori and I were on the outs. Tori has cheated on me numerous times and I thought this was another one of those times. I didn't want to be with her. Then I found out I was wrong—that she hadn't cheated—and things got complicated. I was feeling guilty when we got engaged."

"So, what? You decided to lead me on after that?"

"It's not that simple, Nadia."

"Yes, it is." Before she can say anything, I raise another question. "Okay, then. What about Camille? Because apparently, you were fucking her too."

"What happened with her was an accident."

I laugh. "An accident." That ends our conversation.

128

I call Jonathan into the room. "Can you escort Miss Morriston out? I don't have time for her bullshit."

It only suspected that Laila had slept with Camille. I had no proof until now. I don't know why I keep opening myself up to being hurt by this woman. I feel like a fucking idiot. I've been trying to brush things under the rug, but the truth is she hurt me and I am not over it, and acting like I am isn't the answer. I deserve so much better than this. Shit, I need to respect myself more.

12

NADIA

Rosa makes a green tea for me and a coconut bubble tea for Olivia. I take the tea upstairs to Olivia and ask her what she would like to do. She asks me if we can go to Six Flags tomorrow. Because I look like I need to have some fun. She's so silly trying to put it on me.

I try to coax her into catching a movie or something more low-key, but she's not having it. As I walk out of her room, she boldly asks if we can take the helicopter. I laugh and say no. It's funny she thinks we can fly at any moment, but funnier that I now have the means to grant that wish. Maybe we should take it. I ask Jonathan to find out if it's feasible. He tells me he will check into it. Olivia throws herself backwards onto the bed and starts kicking her legs excitedly. I kiss her goodnight, go to my room, and pull out my journal. This journal is the best gift that Mrs. Spady ever gave me because it's teaching me to express myself.

Dear Purple Book:

I need to put more effort into building a solid relationship with my daughter and spend less time and energy on the silliness with Laila. There's no reason I shouldn't have brought dinner home to her. I'm not that important in Laila's life, so I don't need to put her or anyone else before Olivia or myself.

Carly showed up on my doorstep and dredged up a lot of dormant feelings. It's crazy how things happen in life. I wonder why she has shown up the way she did. I hope she's not trying to get money. Shoot, it may be more beneficial for me to pay her to go away. And Laila she stresses me the fuck out. I need to figure out what I want with her because I can't keep going back and forth with her. Today my libido got the best of me, no I'm not going to say it was only that. Deep down I figured if she was gonna use me for sex then that's what I was going to do to her. I wanted to be in control of our relationship. I wanted things to be on my terms, but that backfired. I let myself be vulnerable and she exploited it. Love is not supposed to be this hard. Now I'm crying, I don't like this pain.

What is wrong with me? I'm considering paying someone to go away, I'm bitchy all the time, mostly for no reason, neglectful of my daughter. I need to pull my shit together. Yes, that's what I'll do. I don't need to worry about any of these women. It seems that being attracted to women has brought me nothing but bad luck. The best times of my life were with Xavier. Maybe I'm not supposed to be gay. One day, I'll figure it out, hopefully, sooner than later. Anyway, tomorrow is a new day to do better.

Nadia

13

TORI and LAILA
October 2011

When I walk into the house, I don't see Tori, so I run upstairs. Just as I make it to the top, she rounds the corner out of the master bedroom and scares the shit out of me. She rolls her eyes at me. We don't hug each other as a greeting anymore. We are living as strangers.

"Shit, Tori. You scared me."

"Where the fuck were you, Laila? I called your desk, your cell phone—no answer," she says in that melancholic monotone voice that's plagued her since the baby died.

I put my hands in my pockets and approach her with caution, trying to hide my guilt by keeping a straight face. Tori waves her hand to stop me and says, "I mean, damn. I know we are not together, but you don't have to be disrespectful. I called you four times because I have something important to tell you, but—"

I cut her off. "I forgot my phone at the office when I went to lunch with Krystal."

"See, a better lie would have involved Trey because I talked to Krystal. But it's all good. No worries."

She crosses her arms before squeezing past me downstairs. I try to speak, but she dismisses me.

I yell, "Stop. Talk to me, Tori?"

She turns around, looks at me, and sighs. "Do you remember that self-awareness and healing retreat I told you about a while ago?"

"The one you were wait-listed for?"

"Yes. So, I got a call today because someone canceled, so I get to go now and I leave Friday."

"You don't seem excited."

"It's a healing retreat, not a vacation. And you stress me out."

"I didn't mean to."

Tori doesn't respond, turning away from me and going into the living room instead. I wait a few minutes then follow behind her.

I sit on the couch next to her. We are close enough to cuddle, but I make sure not to touch her. I curl my knees to my chest, lay my head on them, and look at her. She rolls her eyes then looks away from me, letting her eyes drift into the blackness of the TV screen. She mumbles, "You get on my nerves."

I pick the remote up and find something to watch. *Today turned into a hot fucking mess. I went to visit*

Nadia because I was feeling lonely. She always listens to me vent and I thought that I would be able to ease an apology in there and we could figure out how to have a platonic relationship, but when I saw her with that woman, this jealousy bomb went off in me and I wanted to know if she still desires me, which is fucked up because I really want to be with Tori, even though it does not seem like it. We've been together for so long and owe it to each other to work on things. From this moment on I am don't with Nadia and Camille.

Halfway through the movie, Tori starts drifting in and out of sleep. I ask her if she wants to sleep upstairs tonight.

She shakes her head no. "I'll go downstairs."

I grab her hand and say, "You don't want to stay and finish the movie?"

She jerks her arms from their crossed position and pushes up from the couch.

"No. I'm beat and I have a lot to do tomorrow."

"Do you want me to come down?" *Please say yes, I know what I want now. Well, I've always known what I wanted. I was just being stupid.*

She smirks like she's trying not to frown and then she looks away.

I say, "Okay, maybe tomorrow." *Don't let her tell you no, don't let her shut you out.*

"Night, Laila."

I watch TV for ten more minutes then go upstairs. I call Trey and ask him to be at my house at 6:30

tomorrow morning to help me cook breakfast for Tori.

"Are you sure you want to do that Laila? You can't be too pushy."

"I'm sure. She's leaving for two weeks."

"Where to?"

"Costa Rica."

"Really?"

"Yeah, she's going to that healing retreat."

"I honestly think time apart will do y'all some good. It will give you time to figure out if you really want to be in a relationship with her."

"I have come to the realization that I do, and I only want to be with her."

"That's the thing. Is she really coming around or is she just being nice occasionally?"

"I think she's really coming around, and I truly love her."

"I know you do, honey, and I'm not trying to upset you. It's just that you all have been through a lot. For sanity, both y'all's sanity, it may be best to let it go."

"I can't, I won't." My voice quivers.

"I didn't mean to upset you."

"I know. You always try to tell me the truth."

"But I didn't mean to make you cry."

"I know."

"Well, honey, try to get some sleep. I'll see you in the morning."

* * *

When Tori opens her eyes, I'm standing in front of her with crab cake eggs benedict, a mimosa, and sliced strawberries drizzled with Nutella.

She sits up on her elbows and wipes the sleep from her eyes. "Did you make that?"

"Trey came over and made it."

"Is he still here?"

"No."

She says stoically, "Oh, I was wondering when you learned how to cook."

"Ha, ha." I sit on the bed and feed her a strawberry. "I'm going to take you on a date today, okay?"

"Laila, you don't—"

I place my finger against her lips. "No talking your way out of this." I feed her another strawberry.

"We're going shopping for your trip, then to dinner. I spent all night researching the island and what you'll need for the two weeks you'll be gone."

"Laila, the resort will have most of everything I need."

"I know, but you need clothes and new luggage. We'll discuss that later. Let's enjoy this good food Trey cooked for us."

Her eyes fixate on the plate and stay there the entire time we're eating. When we finish, I take advantage of the situation and crawl under the covers with her. I let myself fall asleep because I know she won't wake me. When she tries to move, I wrap my legs around her. Eventually, she relaxes and holds me like she used to. We lay in bed until about 10:30, when she whispers that she has to pee.

Once she finishes her morning routine of peeing, stretching, brushing her teeth, then washing her face, which I haven't had the chance to witness in more than four months, she leans against the doorframe and says we need to have a serious conversation.

I get excited. "Okay, love. Can we talk about it over dinner?"

She looks down, "Ummm."

I scramble out of the bed. "I'll go get ready for our day."

Tori takes an extra-long time getting ready. When she comes upstairs from the basement again, she says, "Laila, we need to talk."

"Do you want to do it while we shop?"

"No, we need to talk now."

"What is it, love?"

"Come sit with me."

We sit down and she comes straight out with it. "I want to separate. But before you say anything, hear me out."

I frantically shake my head. "No."

"Laila, we've been through a lot over the years, and a lot of our heartache has been because of me. I cheated repeatedly and you stayed."

"Because I forgive you."

"I've torn you to pieces emotionally and this was before the incident. You are a beautiful, brilliant woman, and I've not cherished or loved you the way you deserve."

"That's not true."

"It's true, and the thing is, I'm in a fucked-up place emotionally and mentally, and you deserve better. You deserve to be in a healthy relationship, and I can't give you that because I'm not healthy."

"Victoria stop. You don't need to— I want to be with you."

"Laila, I've been thinking about this for a while and I need some time to work on myself, and if I stay with you, I'll just bring you down."

"Tori, I know we are in a really, really tough spot right now, but we can work... get through this."

"Laila, I can't... I don't... I can't do this anymore."

"No, Victoria. You aren't going to take my life away from me. You don't get to decide what's too much for me. When you cheated, I never abandoned you. I have given you everything, and now you're just like fuck you? No, we are going to work this shit out."

She yells, "Laila, at some point we have got to stop this... this... I don't even know how to describe it."

"Stop trying to run from me."

She comes over to the couch and drops to her knees.

"Laila, don't you see what I've done to you? You've never been a cheater, but I drove you to be one. I put you through hell, and it's not getting better." She looks like she wants to cry, but the psych drugs for her depression won't let her get too emotional.

I say, "Love, we can make it through anything... stop shaking your head."

"Laila, I can't. I've tried, but I feel—"

"You feel what, Tori?"

"That I can't do this."

"Tori, try to explain to me what's going on and we can fix it."

"Laila, I can't. And I didn't tell you, but I'm flying out today because I knew this would be hard, and I didn't want you to start freaking out."

I'm silenced by shock.

"Laila, I don't want to be with you." She gets up to walk away.

"Don't do this, Tori. We are a family. Don't do this."

"I'm sorry, Laila. I'll move as soon as I get back."

"No! We're not breaking up."

Tori gets upset. "How many times have I cheated on you, huh? How many times?"

"It doesn't matter. I forgave you."

"But why? Why do you keep torturing yourself?"

"I'm not. People go through tough times, and I want my tough times to be with you."

"Well, I feel like I need to be alone to get myself together."

"I've given you that space, Tori, and I can continue to."

"Right, but you giving me space included cheating on me. And I'm not mad at you for cheating. I just think it's counterproductive to our individual well-being if we stay together."

I get angry. "Then, I guess this is it, huh?"

Tori gives me a look of apology, takes the engagement ring out of her pocket, and places it on the counter.

"Tori, don't do this."

"I'm sorry, Laila."

"Tori, don't do this."

She walks out on me.

I break down.

14

NADIA

When Olivia comes into the house from dance class, I give her a big hug.

"How was class today?"

"It was good. I had fun."

"Great, I'm glad."

"Ma, I've been thinking—that maybe I can, umm... go to a private school when school starts."

"Jonathan and I talked it over, and I want to go to a private school because I have a driver and Denise has a driver and she said she goes to private school and I probably should too."

I say yes, and we end up talking for an hour about what it was like for her at public school in Pennsylvania. Then she asks me if I'm going to start school in the spring. I didn't realize that she remembered me trying to go back to school before the divorce. It was something that Xavier and I talked about often. I think about it for a while and realize that if I'm going to keep this fortune, I need to learn how to manage it.

"Why not? Go get your laptop, and meet me in the library."

After an hour of searching the internet for private schools, Livey starts browsing the bookshelves. After not being able to find a book to read, we decide to watch Harry Potter. Jonathan goes to the store to buy all the Harry Potter movies he can find. Olivia continues to browse the bookshelf while I play on the computer. Olivia begins to ask questions about Mrs. Spady that I don't have answers for.

"Did Mrs. Spady adopt you, like you and daddy did me? Is that why she left you all her money and stuff? I wish I could have met her."

"Me too love. She would've liked you."

"Really? Did you tell her about me a lot?" Olivia turns around to look at me.

"All the time."

"So, is she sort of like my grandma?"

I think about it for a minute then say, "I guess so. Family is about more than blood, and I saw her as my mother, so yeah." After that, her questions slow, and I get lost in the computer again for about three minutes.

"Was she nice to you all of the time or only sometimes?"

"Just about all of the time."

"Grandma said, 'Everyone who is adopted doesn't have nice parents like me.'"

"That's true."

"Was she gay like you?" That question makes me focus all my attention on her.

"No, she was married to Byron, remember?"

"Yeah, I know, but you were married to daddy and—"

"Olivia, what made you ask me that?"

"Well in this picture she is kissing this lady that looks like you."

I jump up and go around the desk. "Let me see. Well, I'll be damned." Jonathan walks through the door with DVDs and books. I tell Olivia to start the movie and I'll be back after talking to Jonathan.

I grab him by the elbow. "Am I in trouble, Miss Nadia?" he asks.

"No, but we need to talk." We go into the dining room and close the doors.

"How long have you been working for the Spady family?"

"About ten years."

"Was Mrs. Spady a lesbian?"

He smirks, "Umm, not fully."

"What, bisexual?"

"Yes."

"How come no one ever told me?"

"She couldn't handle talking about Naida, and she knew you would be full of questions."

"Hold on! Naida? She said something about her in the hospital. What do you mean stuff she didn't want to talk about? What about her being gay? Who is Naida?"

"It's more complicated than that."

"How?"

"Miss Nadia, I need to go get something, and then I'll be right back. I promise."

I squint my eyes in that don't-bullshit-me kind of way. He says, "Miss York, it is extremely important!"

"Don't think you're going to skate out of this."

"I'll be right back."

When he leaves, I go to the library and find Olivia sprawled out on what was Mrs. Spady's favorite couch. I pick the books up and then walk Olivia upstairs to her bedroom and explain that I have some business to attend, and so I can't watch the movie with her. She starts whining that I always have business and she is my business too. I comfort her by promising to make it up to her tomorrow.

When Jonathan comes back, he has a black square box with him. It has silver trim around the edges, two leather straps, and in between the straps is a metal clasp secured by a small lock.

Jonathan says, "Miss Nadia, everything you need to know is in this box."

"Who is Naida?"

He taps the box, pulls his necklace off, slides the key off the chain, and hands it to me. I always wondered about that key.

"Nadia, take your time and go through everything. Miss Spady told me to tell you—" He stops his sentence while pulling out his wallet. From a small slip of paper, he reads, "Nadia, this box was packed with love. Please try to forgive us and remember to love unconditionally."

I begin to shake. Jonathan gives me a hug and asks if I want him to give me a minute. I nod my head yes. I stare at the box for a long time before I open it. Inside, attached to the lid, is a note that reads, "Nadia, hopefully, this box has found you in great spirits. If it hasn't, then maybe it will bring a little peace to your life. You have never been forgotten. Love, Naida."

Inside the box are letters, pictures, a ring, perfume, five bundles of cash, birthday cards, and a bunch of handwritten pages. A note attached to the bottle of perfume reads, "Nadia, this is the last bottle of perfume Naida Marie purchased before passing on. I thought you might want to know how she smelled." I spray a mist of what smells like a soft pillow of flowers bursting in the air after a spring rain; the soft smooth smell overwhelms me. I sink down to the carpet and sob.

Jonathan comes into the room and lifts my limp body from the floor. I sit up and blow my nose. Jonathan holds me and tells me to let it out.

Through teary eyes, I see Rosa sit on the sofa and grab a pillow.

"Why did they do this? Why didn't she tell me... It's not right... It's not right." I hit the floor with my fist. Why didn't she tell me Naida was my mother? Why did they leave me like this? How come she didn't tell me?" Jonathan strokes my hair in a fatherly way.

"I know, Nadia, I know."

"This is all fucked up. Wait, wait, were they married or whatever, does that make Mrs. Spady my stepmother?"

"Mr. Spady, Mrs. Spady, and Naida were all in a relationship together, well kind of, I'm not sure how long they were together." He becomes flustered for a moment and shakes his head. "Anyway, Mrs. Spady did what she thought was best. She didn't think she was strong enough to tell you. She loved your mother and Mr. Spady with every bit of herself and she wouldn't have been able to stand you hating her because she did not find you sooner. She needed your love and wanted you to feel what it's like to be loved."

I lie down and cover my eyes with my arm. "Even still, she should have told me. Was this like a big fucking joke to you all?"

"Not at all, Miss Nadia. She wanted to tell you as soon as she verified your identity, but she didn't want things to get weird between y'all."

"Verified my identity? How did she…"

"She got a DNA test using your hair."

"What? When?"

"At the hotel."

"What the fuck?"

"Mrs. Spady and Miss Corprew started putting the box together for you about eight years ago."

"Why didn't they just come get me?"

"They looked for you for years and it was nothing but the Lord that placed us in that restaurant that day."

"So, y'all were looking for a while?"

"Yes, we had been going to Pennsylvania every other weekend looking for you. Why don't we put this stuff up for the night and tackle it with a fresh mind tomorrow? It's a lot to take in."

"Am I related to you, Jonathan?"

He laughs. "No! I'm just an employee."

I blow my nose.

"Come on and let me put you to bed."

I follow him upstairs, but I lose the sleep battle to restlessness. I pace the entire house for hours, sometimes checking on Olivia, sometimes stopping to stare at the black box, but never entering the room with it.

15

NADIA

The next morning, Rosa wakes me up with breakfast in hand. After I have eaten most of the fresh spinach and fruit, she brings the box into my room and tells me to go through it slowly. There is a photo album filled with hundreds of pictures. I look like her, especially when I smile. We both have a dimple in our right cheek.

Mrs. Spady and Naida looked happy together like they'd found true love like they were the only ones who mattered to each other.

I study the pictures for almost two hours before flipping through the stack of handwritten pages.

Before I get a chance to examine them, Olivia comes on the intercom and asks me to sit with her while she eats.

Olivia asks me if I've found a school to attend. I tell her I will as soon as I get a chance. She then tells me that she wants to go to school close to D.C. When we finish breakfast, Jonathan takes her to tutoring.

When I walk into my bedroom, papers are everywhere. I left the window open and the wind has scattered what must be a hundred pages. For a second, I think about calling Sandra, my other maid, to pick them up, but my conscience prevents me. I'm capable and that would be fucked up to do. I have to remain grounded and not act as rich as I am.

It's kind of funny if you think about it. I have so much money that I can fly to Pittsburg, say fuck you to Xavier, and fly my ass back before Olivia's tutor leaves. This house has ten fucking bedrooms, fourteen bathrooms, a guest house, and a helicopter pad. I have more than I need and want, but it's not enough to bring back the woman who wrote all of these damn pages, the lady I've wanted to know my entire life. Money can't fill the void of knowing my mother was one state away.

I fly into a rage. Jonathan comes in and tells me to let it all out and that he knows it's tough having to digest all of this. After talking for a while, I ask him the question that's been floating around my head since last night.

"Which room was my mother's?"

"The one across from the library." I get up and run downstairs. I have explored every room in the house since it became mine, but standing in front of this door right now, it feels like I am about to enter into a foreign land. I hesitate before opening the door. When I finally do, all the courage I built up was for nothing. Everything is the same as it was a week ago. The expectation I had of entering a space once owned by my mother goes unfulfilled. It's just a room filled with mundane things. I sit on the bed and ask Jonathan to join me. Jonathan offers me small details about the furniture, like which of the two chairs in the room was her favorite.

I quietly listen for a while and then whisper, "I can't stay here."

Jonathan gives me a puzzled look.

"I can't stay here. Have Rosa pack bags for me and Olivia."

"For how long, Miss Nadia?"

I'm so overwhelmed. I don't understand why Mrs. Spady didn't tell me about this. I'm don't want to stay here, I can't stay here, knowing that my mother used to walk these halls. My heart begins to race. "You know what? Call a realtor. I need to sell this house. It will be too heartbreaking for me to stay here."

"Would you like to find somewhere else to live first?"

"I have my condo."

"Are you sure you want to do this? It's a bit hasty."

"Jonathan, I can't stay here knowing that my mother left me pretty much destitute while she lived it up."

"I don't think that was her intention, Miss Nadia."

"How would you know, Jonathan? You have no idea. You don't know what I've been through."

"Okay, okay, you're right. What do you want me to tell the staff?"

Honestly, they were the furthest thing from my mind, but he's right. I do need to think about the staff. I am responsible for more than Livey and myself. I have a staff I need to keep employed and paid.

"Tell the realtor I need a place close to D.C., near Bethesda, that has no more than five bedrooms, and make sure it has a pool, and a park nearby with running trails. And set an appointment with the accountant."

"Anything else, Miss Nadia?"

"No, that's all."

"Are you sure you don't want to think about it a little more? You shouldn't make emotional decisions."

"No, this house is way too big anyway."

I pace back and forth for a while trying to get my thoughts and emotions together. I need to talk to someone. My first instinct is to call Laila but deep down I know that is not a good idea so I walk outside to the gazebo and call Carly. I ask her if she is available to come over. She says she can't until later tonight. I ask Carly where her girlfriend is. She tells me she's out of town. After getting off the phone with her, I call Laila.

"I haven't heard from you in two weeks, Laila, what have you been doing?"

She laughs and sarcastically says, "Yeah, Trey said I should stop calling you."

"He's a ball-and-chain type of friend huh?"

"I was waiting for you to call me for a quickie."

I try to hide my pain and match her sarcasm. "Oh, so you're down for that?"

She sighs. "Oh, Nadia. You're changing daily, aren't you?!"

"Well, that's a part of life, Laila."

She tries to keep a loving tone. "Is there something you need?"

I let go of my façade and snort through tears and sobs. "Lai, I'm hurting and it sucks because you're partly the cause, but despite that, I miss you terribly, and it seems like ever since that incident, a lot of random stuff has been happening in my life, and I don't know why. I thought we were on the road to a relationship and you fucked me over. It's like throughout my whole life I've been left with unresolved issue after unresolved issue. I feel myself turning into an angry black woman, and deep down I know not everything is your fault, but I want to blame you because I don't have anyone else. Everyone always leaves me."

"Shhh, shhh. Stop crying, honey. Take a deep breath."

I inhale hard to clear my nostrils. "Why did you do this to me?"

"Where are you?"

"At home."

"Okay, I'm gonna leave work and come over."

"No, you don't have to do that. Don't leave work."

"Are you at the Ellicott house?"

"Yeah."

"I'll be there soon."

Our call ends.

* * *

An hour later, Rosa alerts me over the intercom that Laila is here. I tell Rosa to escort her up. I quickly dunk myself in the water and wet the rest of my hair. She loves the way my hair curls when it's wet. When I thought we were in a relationship, she used to stand and watch me take showers. I suggested she grow her hair long, but she said she doesn't like the texture of her hair when it's long.

When she walks through the door, I reach my hand out and say hey.

She leans over and kisses my forehead in that familiar way I miss. Tears roll down my cheeks.

"I miss spending time with you, Laila. I thought we would reach a place where we would come home to each other. I imagined situations like this where we would just be us, you know?"

She remains quiet and brushes my hair back. I sit up, place my wet hand on her cheek, and press my forehead against hers. "Laila, I fell in love with you, and I know I only got to know part of you, but it was enough to make me not want to live without you."

"I love you too, Nadia."

"But you don't love me the way I love you."

"That's not true. I love you for so many reasons."

I don't feel like being confrontational right now, so I don't challenge her statement, but I know she is not in love with me because if she was she wouldn't have hurt me like this. I ask, "Can you wash my hair for me?" She smiles and then asks where the shampoo is.

It's the small things you don't realize you'll miss so much when you break up. God, I wish I did not love her like this. As she's washing my hair, I confess that I don't just want to sleep with her.

"Nadia, tell me what upset you earlier?"

"I found out who my mother is."

She takes a long pause. "Oh my, are you serious. I mean are you okay?"

"I don't know."

"Tell me about her."

"Apparently, she and Mrs. Spady were in a long-term relationship."

"What?"

"Yeah, they lived together for years, with Mr. Spady."

"Wait were they all together."

Laila's phone vibrates for a third time, agitating the fuck out of me. "Answer your phone."

"No, they will leave a message if it's important."

"You sure?" It rings again. "It could be Victoria."

Laila sighs and rolls her eyes. "Nadia, I am here for you. Don't worry about anything else. Tell me how you're feeling right now."

"I honestly don't know. I'm pissed. Sad. Kind of relieved. Disheartened, because I will never get to know her." My heart starts racing. I want to cry. I change the conversation. "Laila! Do you remember the first time we had sex in the shower?"

"Yes!"

"Do you remember the first time I kissed you?"

"Yes, we almost did it in the hallway right then." She laughs.

"I masturbated right after you left."

"I could hear you through the door."

"Could you really?"

"Yes. I wanted to join you but—"

My emotions are all over the place right now. I want them to wash away. "Do you want to take a shower?"

"When?"

"Right now."

"Didn't you just bathe?"

"I was just relaxing in the water. Turn the shower on, would ya?"

As she undresses, I release the water in the tub, turn on some music, and slowly begin to sway to the sounds of KEM. Laila sits on the built-in shower bench, places her elbows on her knees, and gazes at me. I seductively step in with her.

"What is it, Laila?"

"You may not believe it, but I was actually falling in love with you."

Here we go! This is my chance to finally get her to open up, so we can move past all this nonsense.

"Laila, let's put the BS in the closet and have a serious conversation without having sex and work this shit out—"

"That'd make me happy."

I sit down next to her and stress the seriousness of the situation. "If we don't have a completely honest conversation right now, then this may be the last one we have."

She looks at me curiously.

"Do you understand what I'm telling you? This is your very last chance. I am done with the bullshit."

"I understand."

I get straight to the point. "Tell me why you thought it would be okay to manipulate all of us. That question has been eating me up."

Laila presses the back of her head against the wall, looks up at the ceiling, and sighs, "I was being selfish and, after a while, it was like an adrenaline rush."

Finally, the truth. "Keep going."

"I've always been a pretty stiff person who's mostly done things by the book, and... I don't know. It was exhilarating to do something outside the norm, and I didn't think about how I was hurting everyone."

I interrupt her. "All of this was a game to you, to see if you could win?"

"No. And that's the honest truth. I was trying to console myself, and things went way left. It felt good to feel wanted. I felt like—it was like I had accomplished so much, I had this stable life, but I still wasn't enough for Tori. You helped me start living again. My life wasn't about staying at home and going on the occasional expensive vacation anymore."

"But you didn't have to lie Laila. You hurt a lot of people. And for what, your ego?" It looks like she's crying, but I can't tell because we're sitting in the shower.

"I didn't mean to hurt anyone. I mean, I knew it was a possibility, but I truly didn't think it would blow up like this. I'd planned on ending it with everyone, including Tori."

"Why didn't you?"

"I tried. I'd already moved all of Tori's belongings to the basement, and Camille—I told her a couple of times that we shouldn't take things further than they had already gone, and when it came to you, well I chickened out. I could tell you had feelings for me and I didn't want to hurt you."

"I thought you were just being emotional, *and* you didn't say anything about breaking up after that."

She stares at me blankly.

"Why did you let things go as far as they did?"

"I don't have an answer for you, Nadia."

"That's because you knew you were playing games."

"You're right. I can't and won't offer you any excuses. Everything happened so fast. I went from being monogamous to being the cheater of the century."

"It's not so much fun anymore, is it?"

"I didn't mean for any of this to happen." Now she is sobbing. I want to embrace her, but I stay glued to the shower wall. She doesn't need to be comforted; she needs to feel the anguish of her actions.

I ask, "But why did you say yes to being with me if you knew all of this was going on? I trusted you."

"Because I didn't want to disappoint you. I couldn't explain *not* being with you, and I know how bad you wanted to be in a relationship."

That pisses me off. "Don't put this on me. I would never want to be in a relationship built on lies. All those fucking times you asked me 'not to give up on you' because you were in the 'midst of change' and shit. I guess you telling me that I'm not like anyone you've met before was a lie too? I believed you, Laila, I believed you." Feeling dejected, I step out of the shower and say, "I thought you were sincere. I fell in love with you, and you fucking chewed me up, spit me out, and then on top of it all, you humiliated me publicly." With even more sadness in my voice, I say, "I finally took a chance and decided to open up and be with a woman and you broke the little piece of heart I had left.

I struggle to keep it together. "You know how hard it is for me to open up to people, and you made me trust you, Laila, and that's what hurts the most. You made me betray myself. I thought about doing some really fucked up things to you. But, at the end of the day, that would only cause me guilt, which would haunt me more. And to know you did all of this for fun and games. You can't play with people's hearts and expect them to go away quietly, Laila."

She yells, "I'm sorry, Nadia! If I could take it back, I would. I was hurting more than I thought and... and —"

"You decided to hurt others."

Laila pleads. "No, that wasn't my intention. I wanted to take my mind off of Tori, and things progressed further than I thought they would, but I genuinely love you. My relationships with Tori and Camille have nothing to do with the way I feel about you."

"But you only gave us part of you. None of us fully got to know the true Laila, and now you're just that two... excuse me, three-timing bitch that upsets me every time I see you."

"What do you want me to say? I can't take any of it back, and I'm trying to fix this, but you won't let me."

"You are a piece of fucking work, you know that. Trying to flip the tables and make me feel bad."

"I'm sorry Cam —" Laila cuts her statement off, realizing the grave mistake she's made.
I hit the shower door. "Really, Laila?! You call me Camille?! Of the two of them, you mix me up with Camille. You could have at least said your main girl's name. Fuck, woman. I swear to God I regret ever meeting you."

She gets defensive, "So, why then do you still want to fuck me if you regret meeting me?"

Angrily I yell, "Cause your ass is good in bed and until I can find someone else to fuck, why the hell not?"

She gets up and leaves the shower. I yell, "Where are you going?"

"Away from here. I'm done with this conversation. You're not gonna use me."

Instead of backing down and re-adjusting the conversation back to an adult state, I decide to antagonize her. The anger I have erupts.

"Oh! So, because you're done, that's supposed to be it?"

Laila attempts to put her shirt on while giving me the silent treatment. I try to take it away. When I feel one of my nails breaking, I let it go. She grabs her shoes and walks to the staircase, putting on what she can along the way. I wrap a towel around myself and chase behind her, antagonizing her with each step. "What? You can't handle being called out, is that it? It's not fun to get a taste of your own medicine is it, Laila?" We descend the twenty steps into the living room, I follow her out the front door, and we square up in front of the driver's door of her car. Rosa follows us outside, yelling, "No espera, no espera," and jumping between us. I continue to block the door. Rosa tries to get me to move.

"Don't leave, Laila. It's not nice to leave a woman in her driveway in a towel."

She is pistol hot, but I'm not going to let up.

"Move, Nadia!"

Jonathan has come out, along with two other staff members.

I stare at Laila and try to hide my anger.

"I'm sorry, Nadia. I don't know what else there is to say. I have to go. This isn't good for either one of us."

One of them yells, "Miss Nadia, please come inside. Let her leave."

I wipe my tears away.

"I have to go."

I change my tone and softly say, "Laila, you said you love me. Why don't you come back inside, so we can talk?"

She looks at me with cold eyes. "I can't. This was a mistake. I thought we could salvage something, but I see we won't be able to. Can you please move?"

I look at my staff, then step away from her car and let her get in. As she closes the door, I catch it and say, "Laila, I love you."

"Forgive me, Nadia." She pulls the door closed and speedily drives away, taking my towel with her. The towel is caught in the car door collecting remnants of dust, and I am standing here exposed, naked, and wounded by Laila Morriston again.

16

LAILA

God, I wish I had not gone over to Nadia's. Every time we see each other, it becomes chaotic. I've tried to do everything I can to make amends with her, but she always wants more. I'm going to have to do a complete cutoff.

I call Trey. He answers with a playful, "Wassup, boo thang?"

"Hey, Trey. What're you doing?"

"What's wrong, woman? And don't say nothing, because I can hear it in your voice."

I let out a hard sigh before confessing, "I went to see Nadia and it didn't go well."

"Woman! I don't even know if I want to hear what happened. I told you to stay your ass away from her."

"I know, I know, but she said she needed me."

"Stop with the excuses, okay? Tori needs you. But I guess it's out of sight, out of mind, right? You're still being foolish after all that y'all been through. You're still doing what you want to do."

"Trey, please stop."

"No, Laila! How about you stop with the bullshit?"

"I just wanted to see if we could be friends, that's all."

"Right, right... After your wife has been raped, lost the baby from that rape, and had her wife cheat on her with not one but two people at the same time, and you're still being selfish. I'm so frustrated. I'm about to break up with you."

"Trey, I'm sorry."

He pauses for a minute, "Where are you right now?"

"Going home!"

"Come over here so we can talk face to face. It's time for us to have a come to Jesus."

Sadly, I say, "All right, see you soon."

"Laila, you know I love you, right? That's why I keep it real."

I get off the phone with Trey and think about checking my voicemail, but I don't feel like hearing anyone else yell at me, which is probably what Nadia is doing in the messages. I stop by the store and get some liquor for Trey and me.

When I walk up to Trey's door, it's already open. He rises from the couch, comes over, and embraces me. We hug for a long time. He says, "Come on, friend," while taking the bag from my hand.

From the kitchen, I hear him yell, "Laila, you're not gonna like this conversation."

"I know."

He hands me a mixed drink and settles into the couch beside me. We are elbow to elbow.

"Well, then, Laila Morriston. I won't beat around the bush. Somehow, your life has gotten off track, and we need to figure out a plan for you to pull yourself together. It makes me sad to see you like this. I pray every day that you will get back to your old self."

I smile, but not because I am the least bit joyful. I do it to acknowledge his feelings. I sip my drink, look at the glass, and hold the liquid in my mouth for a while. I throw my head back into the couch cushion and swallow hard.

"Laila, what made you jump off track like this?"
I curl into a ball, tears stream down my cheeks into my ears. "I don't know, things just went haywire when I thought Tori was cheating on me."

"And so you decided to steal the crown?"

Slobber escapes my mouth. "Seems that way, huh?"
He hands me a tissue. "So, tell me what happened when you saw Nadia."
I scoff. "Well, I went over there because... Well... I don't know why. I just wanted to see her."

"What was your expectation?"
I shrug my shoulders.

"You had an expectation and you were let down. That's why you sounded all sad when you called me."

"I want to be friends with her, you know? But she always pushes for more."

"Are you leading her on?"

"No, not really."

"Not really! What does that mean?"

"I mean, the last time I went to see her I told her that we couldn't be more than friends."

"The last time. When was the last time... When was the last time y'all fucked, Laila?"

"A couple weeks ago."

"You said that too fast honey. Don't lie."

"Like two weeks ago." I can't tell him the truth.

"No wonder she wants more. You keep playing with these women's emotions. You know y'all women can't sleep together and then just be friends. That shit's too emotional for y'all. Every time you've told me anything about her, y'all were booed up. Now you want to change the game up, and you expect her to just be cool — "

"But I have told her repeatedly that — "

"Laila, you're the problem here. You need to stop communicating with her. Put yourself in her shoes. She wants things she will never have with you, and you keep fanning the flame of hope. And why isn't Tori on your mind when you're out gallivanting in the streets?"

"She is, Trey. That's why I was only trying to be friends with Nadia."

"Oh my god! I want to shake the shit out of you right now. You had sex with Nadia one too many times to be her friend."

"I know, I know, but..."

"If you know, then why do you keep doing this shit? What do you feel like you're missing?"
I shrug my shoulders.

"You need to figure it out, and you need to be the one to cut off communication with these women because you're the problem. You were bold enough to tie up their emotions, knowing you were in a fucked up place. Now you need to be woman enough to let them go."

Trey removes his hand from my shoulder and leans forward. He pulls my chin toward him.
I try to speak, but sobs come out.

"Laila. Love. I know you're hurting much more than you are putting on. Have you thought about taking medication for depression?"

I shake my head, no and quietly say, "You know taking pills is not my thing."

"Yeah, but this is an extremely trying time in your life."

"I don't think that a bunch of pills is going to help me."

"But they just might. I've been watching you fall apart and... and it hurts me to see you like this."

"I'm sorry."

He matches my whisper. "No need to be sorry. Let's just get you better."

I nod my head yes.

"Give me your phone."

I hand it to him without putting up a fight.

"Unlock it. We are going to call Nadia and tell her that y'all can't be friends."

"Trey, that's not necessary. I'm not twelve. And besides, I think she knows that we won't be talking anymore."

"After all you have been through, it is necessary. Laila, sometimes you reach a place of just having to let go, and right now is a perfect time." He pauses. "Laila, you're in love with Nadia, aren't you?"

"NO!"

"Yes, you are. That makes so much sense."

"I am in love with Victoria and Victoria only."

"Lies, Laila, lies. You are only saying that because it sounds good, but your feelings are tied to Nadia."

"How else would you explain this relentless need to be with or around her?"

"She's a good person. I just thought we could be friends, that's all."

"No, this is deeper than a damn friendship. You and I are the best of friends, and you're not up to my ass like that."

"Call her right now and tell her that all of this is too much and you can't keep communicating with her."

Everything inside me wants to resist, but he's right. I can't keep hurting myself or others. As I dial the numbers, my heart begins to race. Luckily, Nadia's voicemail comes on. My voice cracks. "Nadia, I am sorry for all that I've put you through. If I could take back all your hurt, I would." I take a pause. Trey motions for me to keep talking. "Nadia, I can't give you what you want because I love Tori, so we have to stop contacting each other. I'm sorry. Remember to smile when the sun isn't shining. Goodbye."

I hang the phone up, fall over on the couch, and cry into one of the throw pillows. Trey sits next to me. "It's okay, Laila. It's for the best."

17

LAILA and CAMILLE
One week later

If I could've called out of work again, I would have, but today is the day we're previewing the new Allison Hatch Art Gallery and I'm obligated to be there. The firm's interns will get a chance to see their design work implemented into the brand new building before the gallery officially opens.

I put on the biggest smile I can and step onto the purple carpet. After posing for a couple of pictures, I walk into the grand hall gallery. Upon entering the hall, I'm taken aback by a beautiful baroque style painting. The painting starts on a singular canvas, extends beyond that canvas onto the flat wall before climbing onto another canvas, and then falling off again onto the wall again and again until it disappears into the inside corner of the wall. It's like an exaggerated secret garden flowing like a wave. I get lost in its flow, I want to feel its colors, and float away in the waves to an easier time.

Someone behind me laughs. I pull away from the painting and make my way to the presentation hall finding a seat at the end of a row. This semester's interns are giving a presentation on flaws commonly found after a building settles.

It's amazing how you can put all of your time and energy into working out the kinks, ensuring that everything is perfect, only to discover there was a flaw in the plan.

I'm restless, so I go to the bathroom to freshen up. I'm glossing my lips when Camille comes out of a stall. We haven't spoken in four months.

She pauses for a moment then says, "Hello, Laila." It sends shivers down my spine when she says that. My clitoris pulsates making me grab the side of the sink. I look into the mirror at her standing behind me. She has that seductive look in her eyes, the one that was present every time we fucked each other's brains out.

I say, "Camille, we can't." She checks underneath the stall doors, then walks over and locks the bathroom door.

"Camille, we can't!" She leans in and kisses me while unbuckling her pants.

She weaves her tongue around mine and taunts me by biting my bottom lip.

She whispers, "I know, it's over," while lifting me onto the counter.

She slides her hand up my skirt with one hand and pulls my pump off with the other. She finds the slit in my Spanx shorts and strokes my lips open. She kisses my breastbone. I place my hand on her shoulder. She pulls her body away from me. "You're really not into this, huh?"

I shake my head no.

She zips her pants. I adjust my skirt. She puts my shoe back on.

In that fake British accent she jokingly uses, she says, "Come on me love, let's go look at some art," while helping me off the counter.

We walk to the smallest exhibition hall and sit on a vintage wooden footstool barely big enough for two people.

Camille asks, "What do you see in that painting?"

"Circles."

She laughs and shakes her head, "Abstractly, tell me what you see."

"Colorful circles." I lean my shoulder into her.

"Let me ask you this way: Do you see round objects trying to compress into circles or circles trying to transform into something else?"

"See, that's why I like you, always thinking outside the box. If I was single when we met, you would be the perfect match for me."

"Yeah, and now that you are single, I'm not."

"How do you know I'm... wait a minute. You're not single?"

She casually stands up. I grab her arm with contempt. "Wait a minute, Camille."

I realize I'm talking loudly, so I lower my voice. "You're in a relationship? Didn't you just try to sleep with me?"

Her face scrunches. "Are you judging me? Because I could've sworn..."

"Camille, I'm not judging you... It's just."

"That you're judging me."

"When were you going to tell me that you have a girlfriend?"

"It's not like we've been communicating, Laila. You moved on, I moved on." She shrugs her shoulders. "It's the way life goes."

"But why did you just try to fuck me?"

"I miss your body, and I wanted to see if... we would still connect on that level."

Anger jolts me to my feet. "I can't believe my ears right now."

She reaches for me. "My bad, Laila. That was rude."

I scoff, "Your bad," and walk away. She chases me.

"Laila, I'm sorry."

I stop walking. "How do you know I'm single, Camille?"

"What do you mean?"

"Earlier, you said that I'm single now."

"You have the same lost look you did the night you walked into my strip club."

"What look?"

"I can't describe it, but I recognize it. It's like you were in need of something."

People enter the gallery. I straighten my clothes and rummage through my purse for my hand mirror to check my face. I need to make sure I didn't start crying. Someone walks up to Camille, ending our conversation.

I stalk her on the low for the next hour, waiting for a moment when she's alone, but it never comes.

When I notice Camille leaving, I follow her outside. Before I can catch up to her, she's in the car kissing a woman on the cheek—I presume it's her girlfriend. My heart drops.

When they pull my car around, I hop inside and speed around D.C. looking for a bar.

After four shots of tequila, I drunk-text Nadia.

```
Please   acept   my   apology.   I   luv   u
more than I showd you.
    Laila don't.
Nadia here me out. I miss you.
    Stop
Come on, I miss you
    Don't make me block you.
Fuck  woman,  don't  be  diffult  right
now. I'm apolgizing
    Difficult, you made shit difficult
    when you cheated.
```

I didn't mean to ☹
  Get off my phone
Stop trip and hear me out
  I haven't tripped on you yet.
I'm trying to be cinsere and you being a dick
  You just pushed that last button.
  Every time I'm ready to move on,
  you come at me with some bullshit.
I'm trying to apologize. Don't be spiteful bitch.
  Spiteful bitch, okay I got you.
YOU ARE NOW BLOCKED.
I meant A Spiteful bitch... I wasn't calling you a bitch... sorry.

...

Nadia

...

NADIA, please respond.

...

Nadia, I'm sorry.

I slam my phone on the table, and the bartender's head jolts my way. I gesture for him to bring me another shot, not realizing he probably interpreted it as me being unruly toward him. When he hands me the glass, I ask him to close my tab. After he asks me a third time if I'm sure, I get agitated and answer with an I-will-fuck-you-up stare.

It takes him fifteen minutes to come back with my tab. My eyes do a double-take when I see the $75 total. I grit my teeth and whisper, "What the fuck is this? Are you trying to fuck me over?"

"No, ma'am. The extra fee is for the cab I called for you."

"I ain't ask you to call a cab?"

He points to the sign above the bar. "It's our policy."

"Did I ask you to call a fucking cab?"

"You're drunk!"

I throw my hand up. "I'll call my own ride. Now go fix this shit." I call Trey.

The bartender shows me out and makes me stand on the corner until Trey shows up.

I get in the car and try to control the conversation. "How are they goin' take it upon themselves to call a cab wit out asking?"

"Oh, girl. Your breath is foul."

"I swear, businesses are always trying some new shit to screw the customers."

"What did you drink?"

"A couple shots, but that's relevant."

"By the way you look, I would have called a taxi too. You're slushy as shit right now."

I pop forward in the seat and put my hand on the dashboard. "Trey, my car! I don't want to leave it."

"It's already taken care of. Matt is driving it home. I dropped him off in the parking lot before I got you."

"Thanks."

"You're staying at my house from now on, cause at this rate…"

I cry out, "I'm so fucked up," and bash my palm against my forehead.

Trey tries to grab my hands. "I'm going to help you pull it together, okay?" He shakes my wrist. "Do you hear me? I'm going to help you get it together. Now stop. You are not in this alone."

I hold in my sobs and shake my head at him rapidly.

* * *

Six days later, I faintly hear, "Girl, it's time to get up."

I try to push the sound away with my hands.

"Get up, Laila. We got to go." I crack my eyes open and realize the sun isn't up.

I ask, "What time is it, Trey?" even though I already know, I'm just trying to stall.

"Five. Now get that ass up."

"Where we goi—"

Before I can get out of going, he starts playing "Best Thing I Never Had." I frown.

"Trey, that's not nice."

"Oh, did that make you sad? Good. Now get up so we can run."

I scream, "Why are you fucking with me?"

"Cause you're fucking up. Now get up before I come back with some ice. I know you remember it from day one."

"Ugh, fine. I'm up."

"See you downstairs in ten minutes."

After our walk, we drive past our breakfast spot. For the past five days, I've been living an institutionalized life. I get up at five in the morning, eat a banana on the way to the trail, and walk three miles with Trey. After that, we usually eat breakfast at the same vegetarian restaurant, then go back to Trey's so I can shower and be dropped off at work. Then Matt picks me up after work and finally, I am stuck indoors until the next morning. Okay, it may not be as bad as jail, but still.

When we walk into the house, Matt has prepared breakfast. He holds out a bottle of water. I grab it and sit at the table.

I sarcastically ask, "Why are we changing up the routine today."

Trey shocks me by asking, "Are you ready to go home?" I look across the table at him and Matt strangely.

They burst into laughter.

"What?"

Matt says, "Woman if you could've seen that face. You look like you were about to take off running."

"I know, right? She didn't know what to do."

I stay silent and roll my eyes playfully.

"You need to get the house together before your roommate comes back."

"Yeah, you're right."

"Sooo... Bye, Felicia." He swirls his fork. "'Cause we got something to take care of and you're hindering the process."

I laugh. "Okay." I put my fork down and say, "Well, then, I'll see y'all next week. Can I have my keys?"

"They are by the front door."

18

LAILA
Oct 26, 2011

I'm locking the front door, so my back is to the driveway when Victoria pulls her truck in.
She hops out and walks up to me. "I was convinced you'd already left for work."

I respond, "Well, I'm kind of on a different schedule now."

"I'm glad I caught you."

"How was your trip?"

"Good, really good."

"And how were your weeks?"

I look down and say, "Not so good."

"Sorry to hear that."

I shrug my shoulders.

"Can you go back inside for a minute?" Tori asks.

I look at my watch. I have five minutes to spare, so I oblige her. I've been anxious for her return. I've cleaned the house from top to bottom and purchased new University of Wisconsin linens. I would like for us to reconcile but I am not naïve to the fact that it may never happen.

I try to hide my excitement. "Sorry I missed your calls. I was in the shower. I'm so glad that you're, home though. Tell me about your trip."

"I had a chance to sit down and be introspective, and I learned a lot of things about myself."

"What do you mean?"

"It was just, you know, a time for me to evaluate my life from childhood into adulthood. A way to find methods to help me cope with all the bad things that have happened, and how to recognize the positive things in my life."

"That's amazing, babe. So, we have a lot to talk about then, huh? We can get something to eat if you like when I come home and —"

She stops me from completing my sentence. "While I was there, I came to the conclusion — Well, I don't want to say conclusion... I got some clarification on what I want to happen between us."

Before she can say anything to hurt my feelings, I take a deep breath and say, "Okay, let's go to the living room," while hopping down off of the barstool.

As we make our way to the living room, I start speaking before she can. "Victoria, I love you with all of my heart, and I know I got us in this fucked up situation by getting all caught up in my head and then concocting these faux situations because I didn't want to believe that you were a changed person. All I could see was what you did in the past. I was so blinded by the story that I'd made up that I couldn't even recognize the pain you were in. I couldn't recognize the sadness in your eyes. I didn't want to accept the sincerity you presented me with —"

"I know," Tori says, "but there are things that neither one of us will ever be able to take back."

I nod in agreeance and put my hand in the middle of my chest. Tears fall from her eyes. She stares at me and then she says, "I'm sorry."

I slide my fingers toward her wrist. I intertwine my fingers between hers and say, "Tori, you don't need to apologize, I'm the one who—"

"No, listen to me for a second. I have been in love with you a very long time. I fell in love with you the first time that I saw you, but it has taken me years to be able to give you the love you deserve. I've put you through so many ups and downs, and if I could take back all the stressful moments I caused you, I would. But the only thing that I can do is move forward and continue to grow. I forgive you for everything that has happened these last couple of months."

Tori drops down to her knees and pulls out a silver band with a citrine-colored crystal encased in purple amethyst. She says, "When I saw this ring, I thought of us, and all the good times we've had flashed through my mind. My heart began to race because I was scared that we may not make it, and in that moment, I heard you saying we will be all right. So, I'm asking you, Laila Morriston, to please forgive me, grow with me, and continue to learn with me forever. Will you marry me?"

I drop down to my knees and meet her at eye level. "Yes, Victoria Greer, I will."

She stands up. "Okay, let's go now."

"Yes. Wait. No. We can't go now."

"Yes, we can." She grabs my hand and ushers me to the car.

Ten hours later we are standing in front of the Gay Chapel of Las Vegas. Another three hours later, we are naked with my back pressed against the glass window of the hotel room. My legs are draped over her arms. She is pressing into me as I gyrate my clit against her. I bite her on the cheek and brace myself against the glass.

Seductively she asks, "Are you ready for me to eat your pussy?"

"Eat your wife's pussy," I say. She lowers my feet to the floor and kisses her way down. She places her palms against the glass. I ride her tongue furiously. She reaches her tongue inside me deeper than she ever has. I grab her head, brace myself against the glass and let all my pent up emotions explode out of me. I try to stop it, but I can't. I scream and squirt all over her face. She pulls away from me and wipes the wetness from her face. She lies on the floor and I slide my pussy down her belly. I spread my ass cheeks open and press downward onto her.

Tori tries to hold in her moans as I rock back and forth, but she is forced to let them out when I pinch her nipples. In a whisper, she says, "I'm gonna cum."

"Where do you want to cum?"

"I can't hold it, Laila."

"Tell me where you want to cum."

"In your mouth."

I turn around quickly, put my ass on her face, and suck on her clit. She smacks my ass. Her legs begin to shake. "Oh fuck, Laila."

She does what I've been waiting for, the thing that makes us cum together every single time. She jams her fingers into me, catching my g-spot by surprise, I clamp down on her clit with my lips. Her clit throbs in my mouth and my pussy throbs around her fingers. I collapse in exhaustion.

Her belly pushes into mine when she laughs. "Laila, you came in my eye."

I laugh and roll off her onto the floor. I wiggle up to her face, place my hand on her cheek, and kiss her eyelid. "Sorry, babe. I couldn't help it."

"Laila, we are married," Tori says.

I lean over and kiss her passionately. The rest of the weekend is phenomenal.

19

LAILA
October 31, 2011

I'm on cloud twenty when I walk into work Monday morning. I speak to everyone along my path. When I stick the key in my office door, it doesn't work. I shrug it off and walk to the head project manager's office.

"Good morning, Miss Morriston."

"Mrs. Greer now. I got married this weekend."

"Really? Well, congratulations."

"Thanks."

"I'm happy for you, but we need to talk."

"Sure. My office key didn't work"

"You no longer have an office."

"What?"

"Unfortunately, we have to let you go. Your absences over the past year are reflecting negatively on the company and bringing morale down."

I'm stunned. "You've got to be kidding me."

"Laila, I fought for you, but there was nothing I could do. I've been dreading this moment."

"This is unbelievable."

* * *

John Twit, my work husband, calls security and has them escort me from the property after collecting my access badges. We approach my car and someone is standing there with a box of my belongings.

I scream at the situation, "Are you fucking kidding me?" The young intern looks down at the ground.

I unlock the doors and get in the car. The kid puts the box on the back seat and says, "Have a good day."

I want to flick him off, but I don't because it's not his fault. It's no one's fault but my own. I try to look at the bright side of the situation. At least now I have the time to rebuild my relationship properly.

I shake off the bad energy from work as I drive home. When I enter the house, Tori is making her way upstairs from the basement.

"Hey, love, how was your day?" I ask her.

"It's been interesting."

"Really? Do you want to elaborate?"

"Yeah, sit down for a minute."

She doesn't seem happy to see me, "Okay. Well, let me put my stuff down."

When I come back into the living room, Tori is sitting on the couch with her arms crossed. She slowly turns her head toward me. I pop off my heels and ask what she's thinking. She looks at the ceiling. "I'm wondering how Nadia tasted when she was sitting on your face."

I almost pee on myself. "Excuse me?"

"When was the last time you saw Nadia?"

I try to play it cool. "Probably a month and a half ago. I don't remember."

"Is that right?"

She rises from the couch abruptly and is standing in front of me in less than a second.

"Have you all had sex since she came to the hospital?"

"No. Okay, I think I may have once when I went to tell her it was over."

"Are you sure?"

"Yeah."

She grabs my hand and pulls me toward the basement. My heart rate picks up.

"I have to go to the bathroom," I say.

She squeezes my hand tighter. "Hold it."

As we descend the stairs, I hear faint moaning sounds. When we turn the corner, I fake a laugh and say, "Tori, what are you watching?" Before she can say anything, I see Nadia and myself tribbing on the screen. I almost throw up.

Tori starts clapping her hands. "Bravo, look at that face, Laila. I leave for twenty days, and you were onto the next." She snaps her fingers. "Just like that."

I turn and run back up the stairs in a panic.

Tori yells, "Oh no, you don't," and chases me.

I go into the living room and start pacing. "Where did that come from?"

"Where do you think?" She screams.

"Tori that… that tape isn't recent."

She says, "You know, I thought about that, but then I started thinking. After all these months… Nadia is that connected to you. She is hurt enough to leave this on my fucking doorstep and run away like a little bitch!" Tori's screaming so loud she's almost hoarse.

I start stuttering. "Please, calm down, baby. Listen, listen that was made a long time ago. There's got to be a time stamp."

"There's not. I checked."

I drop to my knees and beg. "Please, listen to me. It's old, I swear."

"Get your lying ass up. I have an idea of when it was made."

"When? Tell me."

"You're really asking that question like you have no idea? Unbelievable."

"Baby, let me find out what's going on."

"I know what's going on. We're getting an annulment—no ifs, ands, or buts. I'm done. I would never have gotten myself caught up like you did, Laila. What the fuck is wrong with you?" She grabs her jacket. "I changed my number already, so don't bother trying to call. I cleaned out two of the safes. You can have the other one."

She doesn't say goodbye, she just walks off with her chest heaving.

I'm in disbelief. "God, can I get a fucking break?"

Tori rushes back into the room. "Don't you fucking cry out to God! God didn't have you running around, fucking every lesbian in town."

I get pistol hot. I just got fired, and now this shit. "You think I wanted to go out and cheat, Tori? You think I wanted to feel this—ugh, I can't even describe it? If you hadn't repeatedly crushed me emotionally then I wouldn't have ever been with anyone else."

"So, this is my fault now. I made you sleep with a stripper. Yeah, you think I don't know about that?"

I gasp.

"Don't act all surprised."

"Shut the fuck up, Tori. You cheated on me. Not one, not two, but three fucking times, and now I'm the fucked up one?"

"But I didn't get caught out there like you did."

"What the fuck, Tori? This is so hypocritical."

"Yeah, it is. But you never had anything blatantly put in your face. I always owned up to my wrongdoings."

"Oh, my God. Don't you hear how that sounds? You still fucked around on me. It doesn't matter how I found out. You cheated, and the only reason I cheated was because I was so use to you doing it that I thought it was the only way to make you stop. I wanted you to know how I felt."

"Well, congratulations for accomplishing your goal." Her tone flattens. "I think I'm going to die from all this heartbreak."

I rush over to her and wrap my arms around her before she can react. "I love you wholeheartedly and I'm done with hurting you. We have been through enough."

Tori tries to pry me off her. I say, "Baby, don't do that. Everything will be okay."

She sucks her teeth and shrugs her shoulders. "Go. I need some time to think."

* * *

I leave the house and start blowing Nadia's phone up. She doesn't answer. I leave so many threats to ruin her in every way imaginable that I fill her voicemail. I drive to Ellicott and try to get past the community gates, but security won't let me. I park down the street, but the police make me leave the neighborhood. I call her phone again, then remember my number is blocked. I chuck the phone toward the passenger side of my car. It hits the window, shattering it. The voice in the back of my head starts screaming, "Go home, Laila. Just go home."

When I get to the house I park in the garage and inspect the passenger window. If it wasn't for the tint I would have glass everywhere. I find my phone under the seat, along with the wallet card that Christina gave me months ago. It reads: You may succeed in making another feel guilty about something by blaming him, but you won't succeed in changing whatever it is about you that is making you unhappy. – Wayne Dyer

That bitch.

20

Not the Conclusion

When I walk into the bedroom, Tori is lying in the bed reading. I gently slide into the covers with her. I kiss her cheek and say, "I'm sorry love. I fucked up bad, but I promise it won't happen again."

She puts the book on her stomach. "It won't happen again? It shouldn't have happened in the first place."

"You're right."

She claps the book shut and sits upright. "What is it with you and these women, anyway?"

"There's nothing anymore, I promise."

"Well, there better not be. We've been through too much for anymore fuck ups from either of us. I forgave you because of my past indiscretions, but this is the last time, I promise you that. And the only reason I'm giving you a pass is because I was unable to have sex for so long, and I know you have needs."

"Tori, I won't dishonor you again."

"Well, I hope you're sincere because if I find out anything else, it's over and I mean it."

"I understand." I snuggle into her shoulder and wrap my arms around her. She picks her book up again. I thank the man upstairs and lie silently. I faintly hear. "I'm forgiving you, but we have a long way to go if we are going to stay married."

I sit up on my elbows, and she continues, "When I was on the retreat, we did a lot of self-evaluation exercises, and so I have a better understanding of who I am now."

"What do you mean?" I curl up closer to her.

"For so long, I've been feeling like my identity only involved you. We met on the day I arrived in town and I was right out of high school. I didn't get a chance to build a life on my own. I didn't get a chance to grow up and explore myself before settling down with you."

"I think about that, too." A tear rolls down my cheek to her shoulder. "I feel bad."

She looks down at me. "Don't feel bad. You didn't do anything wrong. I wanted to be with you, and... the best way I can explain it is—at that age, you don't know what you want or what is best. I basically ran away from home because I didn't want to be outed, and I never had a chance to figure out what I wanted for myself. When I cheated on you, I was looking for something in those women that I wasn't going to find."

"I think I understand."

"A beautiful thing happened on the retreat. I found out that everything I do and want in life, the things that suit me best, are exactly what we have. When I talk about my final moments in life, I think about you being by my side. Do you understand what I'm trying to tell you?"

I nod my head.

"Look at me, Laila. I want us to heal from all of this together. I don't want to lose everything we've built."

"I don't either."

"Okay, good. I want you to change your number in the morning, and not talk to them ever again."

"I love you."

"I love you too, Laila De'nae Greer."

The End
The drama will continue shortly!

Coming Soon

IT'S
COMPLICATED

. . .

Preview of Nadia's Spin-off

Oct 30, 2011

Rosa rushes upstairs into Nadia's room and yells. "Miss Nadia, you have company downstairs."

Nadia rolls over and looks at the clock and mumbles to herself, "Isn't Sandra supposed to be here?" When Nadia's eyes focus in on the numbers, she says, "It's eleven at night. Who is it?"

"Carly! Come, miss, come now."

Nadia groans with agitation, "Tell her I'll be down shortly."

"I think she needs you now, Miss Dia. Carly looks beats up."

"What?"

Nadia grabs her robe and runs downstairs. Carly is sitting on the couch with her hair disheveled, red patches scattered on her face, and her left hand bandaged.

Carly stands up and says to Nadia, "I'm sorry, but I didn't have anywhere else to go."

"I'm glad you came here. Do you need a doctor?"

"No, I'm fine."

Nadia tells Rosa to go get some ice packs, then she leans over to grab a Kleenex from the side table. Carly wipes the snot away from her nose. "I'm sorry to drop this on you, Nadia, but I had nowhere else to go."

Nadia scoots closer to Carly and wraps her arms around her. "Don't worry about that. I'm glad you're safe."

"I don't know what to do, Nadia. I mean, I don't want to go to the police."

"If you aren't safe, you have to tell the authorities."

"Come on, Nadia, we both know it's not that simple."

"But sometimes you have to show people the error of their ways."

"She is already going through a lot."

Nadia lifts her head from Carly's shoulder and breaks her embrace. "What could she possibly be going through to repeatedly do this? And let me see your hand."

Carly tries to hide it under her shirt. "It's fine."

"No, it's not. It's steadily bleeding. I know because I've been watching it. Give it here." Nadia piles a few tissues on the table. She places Carly's hand on top of them and slowly peels the bandages off, revealing a two-inch cut.

"What that fuck, Carly? That looks deep. Did she stab you? We have to get this cleaned up. You need stitches."

"No, I'm okay."

"No you're not, we're going to the hospital and I'm not going to let you fight me on this."

Nadia doesn't go into the hospital room with Carly, but while checking in, Nadia hears Carly make up a story about trying to cut a mango and the knife slipping. Two hours later, they are barely outside the ER doors when Nadia softly rips into Carly.

Carly, I have to ask, "How did you get to the point of lying and excusing Shannon's behavior?"

Carly doesn't have an immediate answer prepared. Keeping up the lies and façade is becoming harder by the minute.

"Shannon has been through a lot these past three years and she's struggling to keep it together. She wasn't always like this, and I'm hoping this side of her will... I don't know... go away."

With agitation, Nadia asks, "Has it gotten any better thus far, Carly? I mean, honestly, has it?" Carly shakes her head no.

"Then what in the hell makes you think she's going to change. Abusers don't work that way, especially if she is not getting help." Nadia says that more harshly than she probably should have. Carly reminds herself that Nadia is only angry because she doesn't know the true situation and remains composed.

"I keep hoping that she will heal, so I keep trying to help her."

"What if she does something devastating to you?"

"I don't think it would go that far."

"But she might. I mean, look at your hand. How much further does she have to take it? How did all this start, anyway? She never showed you any signs?"

Carly sighs hard and takes a deep breath. "None of this started until she was fired after whistleblowing. Then she started drinking heavily."

"But you shouldn't have to sacrifice yourself."

"I know, but how can I leave her after all she's been through."

"But that's not an excuse."

They are silent for the rest of the ride. When they get back to the house, Carly sleeps in Naida's old room. Nadia goes to her room and paces the floor trying to figure out what to do about Carly. When the alarm goes off, Nadia is still pacing. She goes downstairs and waits for Olivia to come down. Olivia comes into the kitchen and asks for a bowl of cereal. She is in the middle of telling Olivia they will be moving to a new house when Carly enters the sunroom.

Nadia says to Carly, "Good morning, hun. How are you feeling?"

"I'm okay, I suppose."

"Listen, Carly, you are welcome to stay here as long as you need."

Olivia drops her spoon into the glass bowl. "I thought we were moving."

"We are, honey. Why don't you go get ready for school?"

Olivia agitatedly asks, "Did you stay here last night?"

Nadia says, "She did and don't question adults with that tone."

"So, what? Is she moving with us?"

"Olivia, if you ask another question—" Olivia snatches her bowl off the table.

"Put it back and pick it up correctly... Don't let today be the day."

She says she's sorry with an attitude while walking away.

Carly laughs and shakes her head. "Women and their attitudes."

"I know, right? I don't know what her issue is."

"So, what did you threaten her with?"

"What you mean?"

"You said, 'Don't let today be the day.'"

"Oh, that I whoop her ass."

"You've never?"

"Like once. She's pretty good. But Carly, I meant what I said. You can stay for as long as you need."

"Thanks, Nadia."

"I'm going to be out for a while. I have to go to South Maryland. Help yourself to what you want and don't hesitate to send Sandra out if you need something. She has the house credit card."

"Nadia, you don't know how much I appreciate this."

"It's no problem. I just want you to be safe."

* * *

Nadia drops Olivia off at school and then decides she is going to purge Laila from her life. She goes to her condo and swiftly searches each room, looking for anything Laila may have left behind. She pulls a box from the laundry room and puts all of Laila's stuff in it.

She's almost out the door when she remembers the thumb drive. After carelessly dropping Laila's belongings to the floor she goes to the master bedroom and takes the thumb drive out of the picture frame. Nadia's plan for revenge is expanding. She makes two copies of the recordings for safe keeping and searches the apartment for a necklace box to place the thumb drive in. When she finds one, she heads to Upper Marlboro. On the way to Laila's, she stops at a flower shop and buys two dozen black roses.

She mumbles aloud to herself, "Laila wants to text my phone with some crazy shit. I got her ass. I've been trying to let everything go, but I'm going to have to shut her down completely. I've had enough of her disrupting my life."

Nadia rounds the corner and sees Tori's truck in the driveway. Her heart begins to race. She parks directly in front of the house and gives herself a pep talk. "I guess this is it. You've come this far. Don't chicken out now." She opens the car door and jumps out with the engine still running. She grabs the box of Laila's items from the trunk and the roses from the passenger seat and runs to the front door. She presses the bell about five times, then sprints back to the car.

Inside the house, Victoria is dusting the ceiling fans in the dining room. She's halfway up the ladder when she's startled by the repetitious ringing. She drops the Swiffer duster and descends the steps. When Victoria swings the door open, she sees Nadia's back and yells.

"What the fuck are you doing?"

Nadia says, "Owww, fuck," after hitting her elbow while getting in the car. Victoria steps onto the porch and kicks over the roses. She's looking down when Nadia peers through the window at her. She throws the car into drive and screeches off.

Victoria follows the car with her eyes until it's out of sight, then picks up the box and flowers. She throws the broken vase, including flowers, into the trash and places the box on the counter. Her gut tells her this stuff is for Laila, so she calls her on the phone. Laila doesn't answer; Victoria decides not to leave a message. Trying to ignore the box, Victoria goes back into the dining room to dust. She climbs the ladder and her stomach churns.

Her initial impulse is to ignore the contents of the box is slipping away. Anger, more than curiosity, pulls her toward the box. She spins it around and bites her fingernails. Suddenly, she yanks the flaps apart.

On top of a t-shirt is a white necklace box. Victoria slides the top of the box off, revealing a gray and red flash drive. She flips it over a few times but finds no markings. She goes to her computer and opens the single MOV file.

*

Nadia's still feeling the adrenalin rush when she pulls into her own driveway. She rushes into the house to find Carly on the terrace. The plan was to tell Carly about her bad deed, but she rethinks it when she sees Carly's bandaged hand.

Nadia asks, "How's your hand?"

"It's okay."

Nadia can't ignore the somber look on Carly's face. She knows why Carly is down but asks anyway, "What's on your mind, Carly?"

"Well, I did a lot of thinking last night and came to some hard conclusions."

"You want to share?"

"Well... I called Shannon and told her I'm done."

Nadia takes a seat to show Carly she is fully invested in the conversation, but her thoughts are split. She can't stop thinking about the way she fled from Laila's, but deep down she knows why. She has never dealt with confrontation well, which is why she avoided Carly the last two weeks of high school.

Carly sits next to Nadia, who asks, "How'd she take it?"

"Horribly. We argued for an hour and a half before she finally agreed to go to rehab after I told her we have a chance if she gets therapy."

"Do you think she will?"

"Hopefully she will. It's the only way I'm going back."

"I hope you stay true to that."

"What do you mean?"

"I'm going to be frank, so don't shut me out... I remember how you like to ignore people when they get too serious."

Carly looks puzzled for a second but then laughs. "I try not to do that anymore, for your information."

Nadia smirks and stands up, then crosses her arms in front of her chest.

"Carly, you and Shannon are broken, and if you go back, statistics show that it won't get better."

"That's the thing, though. It could."

Nadia huffs.

"Going back would be like jumping back into hell after being pulled out."

"Damn, Nadia, that's extreme."

"You got my point, though."

"You just don't understand her. She didn't always do this stuff."

"But she does now. This is who she is now, Carly, and it's going to take a lot of therapy to fix it."

Nadia rushes over to the couch and grabs Carly's hands as she drops to her knees. Carly straightens her posture. They look into each other's eyes for a moment.

"Carly, listen to me. You don't have to settle. If you are anything like I remember in high school, you are girlfriend material, so I'm sure you'd have plenty of prospects to help get you through."

Carly wants to hide how flattered she is, but her cheeks flush and she lets out a soft laugh.

Nadia gently guides Carly's chin forward so their eyes can reconnect. "Don't be shy, Carly. It's true."

A tear rolls from Carly's right eye and she softly says, "I've missed talking to you, the way that I treated you has been heavily weighing on me for years. I'm sorry that I hurt you the way I did." Nadia leans back onto her calves, and then quickly shifts to Indian style. "Back then, I was worried about my reputation more than anything, and I didn't understand the impact of my actions. Even now, sometimes, I can be… a little selfish."

"It took me a long time to get over what you did."

"I've never forgiven myself."

"What I couldn't understand was why you turned your back on me when you were the one who initiated things."

Sounding defeated, Carly admits, "I don't have an answer for you. I just caved under the pressure, I guess."

"You did more than cave. You provoked a lot of my teasing. You wouldn't even acknowledge that we were friends. You were the closest person to me and you knew that."

"I'm sorry, Nadia. I was young and stupid."

"I know that. That's why I'm not holding it against you."

Carly starts to respond but she's cut short when Olivia bursts through the door, returning from school. Nadia stands up and braces for Olivia's daily hug.

"How was school, baby?"

"It was good... I see your friend is still here."

"Does that bother you?"

Olivia shrugs her shoulders and heads upstairs. Nadia yells, "Get back over here. Don't walk away from me like that." Olivia returns to Nadia with a lackadaisical attitude.

Olivia mumbles sorry. Nadia asks her again, "Does that bother you?"

"No, but is she your girlfriend?"

"She is not my girlfriend. She is my friend who needs my help."

"Oh."

"Baby, I will tell you if I start dating someone."

"Okay."

"Listen up, though. I'm not going to let you be disrespectful to people, okay? That was very uncalled for this morning, and a moment ago."

"I'm sorry."

"Just don't let it happen again. Go ahead upstairs. I'll be back down in a little while Carly, so we can finish our conversation."

In Olivia's room, they lay across Olivia's bed and Nadia asks, "Does it bother you that I am a lesbian?

Olivia shrugs her shoulders.

"What does that mean? Open your mouth, baby."

"Daddy said you're going to hell because of it."

"I'm not going to hell because I'm a lesbian."

"But the Bible—"

Nadia cuts her off, "The Bible says God is love, so as long as I love and not hate, I think I'll be okay."

"So is Daddy going to hell because he hates lesbians?"

Erika Renee Land

Nadia starts fidgeting and thinking hard. "Okay, Olivia, look at me. I have no idea what is going to happen, but I do know that as long as you..." Nadia softly presses her finger into Olivia's chest. "Do the right thing, you will keep God's favor. Do you understand?"

"Yeah."

"Do you really understand, or are you just saying that?"

"I understand."

Nadia changes the subject by telling Olivia to change her clothes.

"Did anything interesting happen in school today?"

"No. Same old, same old." That makes Nadia laugh.

"Same stuff, different day, huh?"

Olivia smiles. "I have to do my homework."

Nadia leaves Olivia to her homework and returns to the kitchen. Carly is eating a bowl of grapes. Nadia says, "I want you to stay here with me for as long as you need okay. I want to work on building a friendship with you."

Every story has three sides! Stay tuned to hear what Tori has to say.

About the Author

Erika Renee Land is a native of Norfolk, Virginia. Upon graduating from high school, Erika enlisted in the United States Army, where she served for six and a half years.

In February 2009, Erika's military career ended, and she relocated to Athens, Georgia to attend the University of Georgia (UGA). Her initial plan was to attend pharmacy school; however, along the way, she discovered a hidden passion for writing and literature. So, she changed her major to English and embarked on a writing career.

During her academic transition, Erika found that writing is more than a passion. It also serves as a therapeutic tool, which helps her cope with Post Traumatic Stress Disorder stemming from her time spent supporting the war in Iraq. Erika started writing poetry to cope with the stresses of PTSD and is 21st century war poet that gives motivational speeches for individuals and corporations about overcoming any setback one may face. Check out her poetry and other writings on her website at www.erikaRland.com. Also, visit the site for author appearances and much more.

Facebook: www.facebook.com/erikareneeland
Twitter: @erikareneeland
Instagram: PoetryNotWar

www.ingramcontent.com/pod-product-compliance
Lightning Source LLC
Chambersburg PA
CBHW072103170626
46813CB00004B/1448

* 9 7 8 0 9 8 5 2 8 3 6 6 7 *